Adeline's DREAM

LINDA AKSOMITIS

COTEAU
BOOKS
FOR KIDS

FROM MANY
PEOPLES

Edited by Joanne Gerber.
Cover images: "Vintage Steam Locomotive," by Blasius Erlinger/Gerry Images and, "The Keary Girls" (detail), London Stereoscopic Company/Getty Images.
Cover montage and book design by Duncan Campbell.
Printed and bound in Canada by Gauvin Press

Library and Archives Canada Cataloguing in Publication

Aksomitis, Linda
Adeline's dream / Linda Aksomitis.

(From many peoples)
ISBN 1-55050-323-5

1. Germans—Saskatchewan—Juvenile fiction.
1. Title. 11. Series.

PS8601.K85A64 2005   jC813'.6   C2005-904907-3

10   9   8   7   6   5   4   3   2

2517 Victoria Ave.
Regina, Saskatchewan
Canada   S4P 0T2

Available in Canada & the US from
Fitzhenry & Whiteside
195 Allstate Parkway
Markham, ON,   L3R 4T8

The publisher gratefully acknowledges the financial support of its publishing program by: the Saskatchewan Arts Board, the Canada Council for the Arts, the Government of Canada through the Book Publishing Industry Development Program (BPIDP), the City of Regina Arts Commission, the Saskatchewan Cultural Industries Development Fund, Saskatchewan Culture Youth and Recreation, SaskCulture Inc., Saskatchewan Centennial 2005, Saskatchewan Lotteries, and the Lavonne Black Memorial Fund.

Adeline's
DREAM

*In memory of our Nana:Adeline
(nee Miller) Agopsowicz.*
— LINDA AKSOMITIS

This book, and the rest of the
From Many Peoples *series
is dedicated to the memory of La Vonne Black.
(See page 206)*

CHAPTER 1

Adeline stared out the grimy window as the empty Saskatchewan prairie rolled by. She swayed with the train's movement, as she had for almost three thousand miles since they left Pier 2 in Halifax, while it banged, clanged, and rattled over the tracks. Feeling Konrad fidget on the narrow seat beside her, she remembered the hard benches where they'd been squashed together in the immigration hall, waiting for their names to be called. Until their papers were stamped, Mama had been sure they might be sent back to Germany.

After learning many English words during the three-week-long boat trip, Adeline had asked hundreds of questions about their new country as they crossed Canada. Now, most of the people seemed too busy to talk. Instead, they tucked their newspapers and books into overnight bags, gathering their possessions for the stop.

She turned back to Mama, and said, "Do we have all our things in the satchel?"

Mama hadn't found the language so easy. She nodded, and replied in German, *"Sitzen herunter,* Adeline."

"I'm so tired of sitting, Mama. Please can I stand?" Adeline peered out the window again. "Our stop is next."

The whistle blew and she flopped back to brace for the final stop. Mama wrapped an arm around Konrad, holding his wiggling five-year-old body still.

At the final screech of the brakes everyone in the rail car scrambled for the door, suddenly anxious to smell the fresh air outside. Adeline leapt to her feet too, both excited and nervous. Her Papa would be waiting for them out there somewhere if he'd received their telegram. She had been staring at his face in its gold frame for four years; now at last she would see him again.

Adeline stepped onto the wooden platform, into a world of swirling dust and heat. Her head spun too, while she wobbled like a marionette with unsteady legs and feet glued to the ground, her body still moving as if it was on the train. People bumped her. People shouted excited greetings. People rushed at one another, hugging happily, but nobody rushed towards them. She clutched Mama's hand to make sure she wouldn't lose her in the commotion of passengers and trunks

In a few moments most of the crowd moved off the train platform, then a man strode out of the shadow of the station building towards them. His sunburnt face seemed weary, his clothes grimy and unkempt. Adeline felt suddenly shy as he neared Mama and smiled.

"Mein lieb, I've missed you," the man said, in German, drawing Mama close with one arm and holding her tightly. With his other hand, he pulled Konrad to him. "What a big boy you've grown into!"

Tears streamed down Mama's face as she ran her fingers over his cheeks, as if to feel that he was real.

Konrad wriggled for a minute, then grinned.

Adeline stepped backwards, trying to hide behind Mama's thin body in the folds of her long navy skirt, but of course she was too tall. After all, she was already twelve, and nearly grown. While she knew the man must be her Papa, he didn't look at all like she remembered. His cheeks had hollows, where they used to be round and merry. The dark hair that had fallen around his face in curls was cut short, and seemed thin, like most of it was gone. This man looked tired, while the Papa who had waved to them from the steamship in Germany four years ago had been full of excitement.

She wasn't sure what to do. Her heart thumped like it would leap out of her chest.

Finally he let go of Mama and Konrad, and turned to her. "Adeline, my Linna, my little mouse," he said, reminding her of the pet name he'd given her for her mousy brown hair. He held out his arms. "You look just like your Tante Karoline."

"She does, doesn't she?" Mama said, her brown eyes glowing under the tight knot of dark hair that crowned her head. She dragged Adeline closer. "She's still a song-bird too, just like Karoline."

Without thinking Adeline said, "But you don't seem at all like I remember you!"

"I guess I don't," Papa replied slowly. He and Mama gazed at her, their hands clasped together.

The happiness on Mama's face faded. "Where are your manners, Linna?" So she was Linna again, now that they had got here safely.

Taking a deep breath, and summoning the manners Mama was proud of, Linna whispered, "Hello," adding as an afterthought, "Papa," but stepped quickly out of reach.

"I guess you're not a little girl anymore," said Papa, a faraway look in his eyes. "Well, let's find your things. I must get back to the mill. It's lucky today is my day for doing the accounts, so I can put in the time easily after everyone else leaves."

He straightened, his shirt's sleeves rolled up and its neck buttons undone, so unlike the Papa she remembered in his dark suit, white shirt, and tie. Nothing had been the same since the day five years ago when he came home and told them the Berliner Bank had been taken over by the Commerz-und-Disconto Bank and he no longer had a job. After that Linna's memories jumbled together. They had left the city streets of beautiful Berlin and moved to Nana's tiny cottage in

Colmberg. Then Papa had sailed halfway around the world to start a new life for them. Now here she was, staring at someone who was her Papa, but wasn't.

Konrad yanked at Papa's shirt, until he finally swung him into the air like he was still a baby. If only it could be that easy for Linna.

She was confused by the mixed-up way she felt at finally seeing Papa again, and by how different he seemed in this new land. Dizzy again, this time from the sun beaming on her head, she sighed. If only she could get to the new house in Qu'Appelle, wash her face, close her eyes, and go to sleep in a real bed, lying down, she would surely feel better.

A few people hovered over trunks the train attendant had unloaded on the platform. Linna spotted theirs, its silver corners shining in the sunlight, and the name MUELLER printed on the long blue tag. She stood back, half listening to Mama asking Papa questions, while she peered around the place that was to be her new home.

A girl about Linna's age walked past, then stopped to stare. She was pretty. Her yellow dress was all frills and lace, and reached almost to her black shoes with their ankle straps instead of laces. When their eyes met the girl straightened, smoothed the folds of her fancy clothes, and strode away towards a lady. She said in a voice loud enough for Linna to hear, "More squatters. They should go back to Germany."

Linna didn't understand all of the English words, but guessed they weren't friendly. She felt a gush of homesickness flood her at the rejection, as she thought about cousin Elli still in Germany. Glancing down at her own wrinkled blue skirt, she held her hand over the small pocket that was really a patch.

Try as she might, Linna couldn't completely ignore the girl. She watched her climb into a fancy black carriage hitched to a horse that pawed the ground; the girl sat between the two adults. Linna expected the man who'd been on the train with them must be her papa, since they both had the same golden hair. The lady, surely her mama, had beautiful copper-coloured ringlets cascading from the back of a blue hat. They seemed wealthy, almost like the Baron and Baroness at Castle Colmberg, where Tante Karoline worked.

Perhaps, Linna hoped, the girl didn't live in the town, and she would never see her again. Or, if she did, maybe the girl would like her once they actually met. She missed cousin Elli terribly, and hoped someone in Canada would want to be her friend.

Several people left the platform, carrying their bags and small trunks across the narrow dirt street to a two-storeyed white building, with *Leland House* on a sign over the big entrance door, and a small second-floor balcony. Linna guessed it must be a lodging house. A lady, her tiny white parasol protecting her from the sun, emerged and waved. Linna turned to see a young man return the wave from the seat of a wagon.

Konrad pointed to Leland House, and said, "Wouldn't you like to go there?"

Linna nodded, thinking of ice-cold water and a large *fettkrapfen,* sprinkled with sugar. Gulp and it would be gone. She smiled, remembering how Papa had always teased her about who ate the hole in the middle of the doughnut.

"When I'm grown I'll build big places like that all over Canada," Konrad said, scraping his boot over the grey boards of the platform.

"Maybe." Linna smiled at her younger brother, so earnest in his best Sunday sailor suit. He had many dreams, just like Papa. One day he was going to do impossible things like fly through the sky, while the next he wanted to be a doctor or drive a train.

"What will you be, Linna?" he asked, grinning.

Linna didn't have to think — her answer was always the same. She wanted to be a singer. After she helped Tante Karoline at the castle when Gisela Staudigl performed Brangäne from *Tristan und Isolde,* she'd become even surer. "A lady who sings in the opera of course. I'll wear fancy dresses and sing every night to crowds and crowds of people." She let her mind linger on the memory of the beautiful singer and her voice.

The creak of a nearby wagon turning abruptly brought Linna back to the hot reality of Qu'Appelle.

It headed toward the five grain elevators towering beside the railroad tracks. She had seen the different coloured giants through the train windows as it rocked its way across the prairies, and had a friendly lady explain their purpose. It seemed strange to think of farmers having so much more grain than they could feed their animals, or themselves, that they needed such enormous storage buildings, but Canada was full of surprises. Some, like Ontario's pine forests and hills, which reminded her of home, had been welcome ones. Others, like the land as flat as a table around Winnipeg, had been almost unbelievable.

The thing Linna liked the least about the prairie was its vast emptiness, which seemed to stretch from the edge of town where she stood, to the sky. She missed home and wished Papa had settled in Ontario. Here, the few trees were scattered and spindly, their leaves small, and there were no pines at all. She wondered how she would ever think of this naked place as home.

"We're ready," said Papa, gesturing towards a small wooden wagon hitched to an enormous black horse with thick legs and huge feet. "I've borrowed this to take you all home. Climb on."

A few people on the platform watched as Mama and Papa carried the trunk between them, but nobody stepped forward to help. Instead, they settled in the shade or entered the station, as if to hide from the hot prairie sun.

As she and Konrad followed, Linna noticed something different in the air. She wrinkled her nose in disgust. "What is that smell?" she asked.

Papa pointed at neat squared fences in the distance. "Stockyards," he answered shortly. A cow bellowed, as if to agree with him.

Thud! Mama dropped her end of the heavy trunk behind the wagon, sneezing as dust flew into her face. When she and Papa lifted it again, Linna hurried to push on the underside, to make it easier for Mama. Konrad tried, but his chubby short arms and legs only had baby strength. Her fingers scraped across the rough surface, as she lifted with all her might. She'd been Mama's helper since Papa left for Canada, so she was used to trying hard.

Konrad wiggled over to make more room for Linna. "I'm helping."

"You sure are," Papa said, grunting loudly as the trunk finally teetered on the edge. "Help your mama and sister balance it while I jump in the wagon, and pull it the rest of the way on."

"We can do it." Mama's voice sounded strained, like it really was much too hard for her.

Linna pushed, feeling the muscles pull right to her stomach. At last the trunk slid across the weathered boards.

Konrad hopped in circles, shouting, "*Gut, gut* – good! I am strong, right Papa?"

"Yes, you made the difference boy," Papa said. He lifted his cap and wiped one hand across his brow, then boosted Konrad onto the back of the wagon, beside the trunk.

Linna rushed to pull herself on, feeling the wagon's rough texture beneath her fingers. She didn't need Papa's help. She and Mama had managed while he was gone. When she stood she saw Mama had already settled on the seat up front.

Linna peered out at the streets leading away from the station, into town. While the nearby buildings seemed to be mostly businesses, she saw a few houses, some brick, but mostly wooden, some tall enough to have two floors. Suddenly she was excited again. Papa had written letters about the house he was going to build, how it would have shiny wooden floors and an upstairs where she could have her own room, instead of all of them sharing the little cottage with Nana beside der Oncle Helmut's family and the big house.

Papa climbed up beside Mama, and took the reins in his hands. "Giddup Ned." Papa clicked his tongue to get the horse moving, and flicked the leather lines. The horse lifted its ears, as if acknowledging his instructions, before beginning to move.

The wagon wheels rolled over the gritty road, squeaking noisily. There were few people left on the streets, just a boy riding his bicycle towards them down the side of the road.

"I'm not sure how to tell you," Papa began, taking one of Mama's soft hands in his own calloused ones.

Mama spoke, as she always did, in her gentle voice. "We're all together now, here in the new country you've chosen to make our home. So, whatever it is, it can't be too big of a problem."

"What is it?" whispered Konrad, leaning over the trunk towards Linna.

"Shhh," she answered, straining to hear over the sound of the train starting to roll down the tracks. But Papa's words disappeared into the clanging and banging, leaving her no wiser than she had been. "Now you've made me miss whatever is happening," she said in frustration, leaning back against the trunk.

"It's so hot," groaned Konrad. "I wish I had some water." His round face was red, and dark curls clung to his cheeks and forehead.

Linna nodded. "Me too. I imagine there will be water in our new house. Maybe we will even have our own stream in the backyard and a vegetable garden tall with plants. Mama would like that."

Konrad puffed and said, "The train ride was long, wasn't it? I hope we stay here forever."

"Much too long," Linna answered, swatting a small black fly that had landed on her skirt. She wasn't sure, however, that she wanted to stay in Qu'Appelle forever. "Look at the nice houses over there. Maybe one of them is ours."

They passed two streets of houses, mostly two-storeyed and painted white. But the horse plodded on, then turned away from the inviting homes, past a large building with a horse and wagon by an open doorway. A man emerged, carefully laying a big bag in the wagon.

"That's the mill," Papa said, turning back to Linna and pointing. "I work bagging the flour there, and do the accounts." Mama smiled, patting his arm.

"Oh," Linna said, too nervous to ask why they weren't heading towards the houses in the town. She'd have asked the old Papa who left Germany, but this Papa seemed so serious. The wagon bumped over the train tracks in the direction of the afternoon sun, towards a strange group of tiny white huts, all trimmed with blue.

Konrad, obviously not as intimidated as Linna felt, moved further ahead in the wagon, and tapped Papa on the back. "What are those?"

"Sod houses, or soddies," Papa said. "Ours is in the last row."

Linna gazed at the sod houses in dismay. She wished she could blink her eyes and see Nana's stone cottage on the banks of the river. If she concentrated maybe she could be back at Castle Colmberg only a kilometre away, where Tante Karoline was a ladies' maid and Linna snuck in sometimes to visit. Where was the new house? Papa had promised her a two-storey house with a room of her own. Tears filled her eyes. These huts were nothing like Papa had written about in his letters.

"They look funny," Konrad said, his voice quivering. "They look like grass grows on top of them."

Mama turned, a strange trying-to-smile expression on her face. Her voice was strained, like maybe she wanted to cry too. "It's wonderful to be here with Papa, children. I'm sure the soddie will be fine."

Linna stared at the little square blocked houses people had tried to make pretty with whitewash. "Sod is dirt, isn't it Papa?" she whispered, more than a little afraid what his answer would be. "Are we going to live in a house of dirt?"

Papa didn't answer.

Konrad's face brightened. "If we live in the dirt, maybe I won't have to keep so clean anymore."

Linna shook her head. She whispered, so low only Konrad could hear, "No, we'll probably just have to wash twenty times every day to keep clean. Papa may have changed, but Mama is still our Mama."

Papa waved at a lady bent in her garden as he guided the horse and wagon through the narrow trail past most of the soddies. He stopped in front of a small square one, with a window on each side of an unpainted wooden door. Corn plants, their new stalks wilted in the sun, stood in short crooked rows next to its west wall.

Mama exclaimed, "We do have a garden! How wonderful." She began to climb out of the wagon.

The garden on the other side of the soddie seemed already baked, with even the leaves of the potato plants drooping onto the dark earth. A green bug leapt up from between the thin stems of grass, and landed on Linna's arm, its long legs prickling her skin. Without thinking, she screamed, shaking her arm to get rid of it.

"It's just a grasshopper," Papa said. "They're everywhere because it's dry this year."

Linna felt embarrassed, and stared down at her worn brown shoes to keep everyone from seeing the flush that surely crept up her face. She wasn't usually afraid of bugs, in fact she and Elli had often pulled weeds in the garden.

Konrad jumped from the wagon, in hot pursuit of the insect. "I want to see it! I want to see it," he squealed.

"You'll tire of them soon," Papa said, grabbing one side of the trunk. A lady, her sturdy body swallowed by a baggy blue dress, emerged from a nearby soddie to join Mama at the handle on her side. With the additional help Linna stayed back, watching Konrad.

"*Willkommen!*" The lady beamed, throwing her chubby arms around Mama once the trunk was on the ground. "Welcome to Qu'Appelle, Frieda. I'm Anke, your neighbour," she continued in German.

A smile broke out on Mama's tired thin face. Those were the first German words they'd heard besides Papa's since the train left Winnipeg, where the last of the friends they'd made on the boat got off.

"*Danke.* Thank you, oh thank you, Anke," Mama said, her eyes overflowing with tears.

Papa picked up one side of the trunk again. "Come, we'll put this in the soddie, then I must go back to work."

Linna dreaded the moment she'd walk through the door behind them, but the sun on her bare head was making her feel dizzy again. Germany had never been so hot. And the wind, what little there was, swept over her skin like a dragon's breath.

Papa swung the door open and backed into the sod house, while Mama and Anke followed, lugging the other end of the trunk. Konrad appeared immediately, darting past them.

"Linna," shouted Konrad, sticking his head back out the door, "It's cool inside. Hurry."

But Linna's feet refused to co-operate. She leaned against the wagon, listening to the wind whisper through the spindly blades of prairie grass. Overhead birds swooped, then darted skyward, like they couldn't find anything worthwhile below either. The loud *caw* of a crow jeered at her, standing alone in front of the dirt house.

Papa emerged, extended a hand towards her, then dropped it. "I'm sorry there isn't a proper house, Linna. I tried, but there wasn't enough money for everything we needed. Soon, I hope."

Linna didn't answer. She glanced up, but quickly turned away when she recognized sorrow and hurt in his eyes. Four years ago she'd have hugged him to try to make him feel better, but today she couldn't. It was hard to even think of him as Papa yet; he seemed so different from the photograph she'd been staring at while he was gone.

"Well mouse – or maybe I should be calling you Adeline since you've grown into such a big girl – I must get back to work," he said, turning towards the wagon.

Mama stepped outside again. "We'll wait to eat until you return tonight. Linna come in out of the sun." Her voice sounded full of authority once again, like the Mama who had brought them halfway around the world.

Linna hurried away from the wagon before it started to move. She had no choice but to follow Mama through the ugly door.

After the brightness of the sunshine, she couldn't see anything inside the dark soddie for a few minutes. She pushed the door shut behind her, leaning against its rough surface, while her eyes adjusted. It smelt like the earth when she planted potatoes with Elli in the spring.

"It's a fine stove you have," Anke said, "with a good big oven and a water reservoir. At least you'll be able to bake bread."

Mama said, "It's so hot outside it would be nice not to use the stove, but to keep it cool."

Anke sighed. "Yes, it has been very warm now for weeks and it's only the last day of June. July is usually hotter yet. It's rained enough to keep the garden growing, but just barely."

Gradually the room appeared brighter for Linna. Anke and Mama stood over the black metal mammoth that filled nearly a quarter of the back wall, peering into the warming oven on its top, like it was something wonderful. The trunk sat in the middle of the single room, waiting, it seemed, for Mama to decide where to drag it.

A few shelves with plates and cooking pots hung from the wall beside Linna, with a tiny table and two chairs nearby. She wondered absently where she and Konrad would sit to eat. On the bed? Perhaps on the dirt floor? She shuddered.

On the right, four steel posts of a white metal bed, covered by a grey blanket with black stripes across the top and bottom, took up nearly the whole corner. On the opposite wall stood a frame for what she was sure were narrow bunk beds for her and Konrad. The walls were dirt – plain dirt, and so was the floor. Linna felt tears threaten. Only animals lived in the dirt.

"I see you already have a pail of water," Anke said, lifting a tin plate and looking underneath it into a shiny steel bucket perched on a shelf beside the stove. "I'll show you where the well is once you're settled. Mind you, there's not much water in this drought."

"*Danke,* I thank you for your help." Mama smiled at her new friend. "I'm sure we'll have lots of questions for you. But now I think we need to settle in and find something to eat."

Anke patted Mama on the arm. "Don't be afraid to ask for whatever you need. We don't have much, but we share what we have. And you," she said, patting Konrad on the head, "once you have some lunch you come and play with my boy Dieter. He's just your size."

A smile filled Konrad's face. "Oh yes. Can I Mama?" Mama nodded.

Linna moved to let Anke through the door. The hot blast of air reminded her the soddie was, at least, much cooler.

"This house is very strange," Konrad said, stooping to pat the hard earth on the floor with his grubby hands.

"It may not be what we expected, but it's where we're going to live for now and be thankful," Mama said. "Once we've unpacked our belongings and spread them out it will feel much more like home." She reached down the front of her dress to pull out the trunk key that hung on a long string.

Seeing the smiles on their faces, Linna's feelings bubbled up and overflowed. "It isn't all right at all! Animals should live in soddies, not people. Papa wrote us about a house where I'd have a room in the top all to myself." A tear escaped down her cheek.

"He's done the best he could," Mama said, her voice soft and soothing.

"It will be fun here." Konrad flopped down on the big bed. "There are lots of new things to see. It will be an adventure."

Konrad sounded just like Papa. But Linna wasn't looking for adventure, she missed Elli and the things she was used to.

"Yes," whispered Mama, pulling Linna into her arms. "We must show Papa we appreciate how hard he's worked to bring us all to this new country, instead of letting us live with your Nana and rely on der Oncle Helmut and Tante Edwina's family. You know their house is full with the children to provide for. It's up to us to help make a home now that we're here."

Linna stood stiffly in the circle of Mama's arms. In a second her stomach rumbled, reminding her that it was already afternoon and she hadn't eaten since a little after sunrise. "I'm hungry," she mumbled, pushing herself away. She was a big girl, and big girls didn't cry all over their mamas.

"Me too," Konrad said, leaping to his feet. "Where is the food in a sod house?"

"We still have a little bread and cheese we brought for the train trip." Mama reached for the large satchel she'd carried with them on the journey. "Come, get a cup and dip yourself some water. We'll rest before we do anything more." Linna looked around, wondering what you did in a sod house to make it a home.

CHAPTER 2

L inna stomped down the dirt path between soddies to the pump that sat at the edge of the little community. The shiny tin water pail banged against her leg with each step, but she ignored the pain, still miserable from the night before. Her first sleep in the soddie had been horrible. The mattress stuffed with prickly straw was not soft, like the feather one she had at home. Every time she rolled over on the narrow shelf that passed for a bed, she'd come face to face with the damp, dark earth. She'd even dreamt she was a long, wiggly worm, and woke with her back pressed against the cool dirt.

But the worst part was waking up in the cramped little soddie knowing she couldn't run up to the big house to play with Elli. Of course they'd had chores to do there as well, but they'd been able to chatter and do things together. Here she was alone. Mama had Papa, Konrad had Dieter. She had nobody.

The morning sun was already high in the clear blue sky. Although she couldn't see anyone, she heard the laughing voices of children. Ugly grasshoppers leapt amidst the grass and gardens, rubbing against her legs as she passed. A robin chirped in one of the few half-grown trees. It was already hot enough that she felt like some wicked witch had pushed her into an oven.

A girl stepped out from a soddie, surprising her. The girl's suntanned legs and bare feet stuck out of a short blue dress, making her seem like a small child even though she was nearly as tall as Linna. It was her hair, though, that Linna stared at enviously. Dark brown, thick curls as glossy and beautiful as that on a china doll she remembered seeing, cascaded over her shoulders and thin arms.

"*Willkommen,*" said the girl. "Hello."

Linna wasn't sure how to answer. She wanted to learn to speak English properly before school began in the fall, but her own language was so much easier. "Hello," she finally said.

The other girl grinned, a dimple appearing in her chin. "I'm Katarine Schaeffer, but everyone calls me Kat. I'm on my way for water – you too, I guess," she said in a mixture of the two languages, while she gestured towards the water pail.

Relieved she would get to practise English, but not have to rely on it, Linna smiled back. "Hello Kat. I'm Adeline Mueller – but they call me Linna. My mama and brother and I just came yesterday."

"I know. My papa told us last night when he came home. He works with your papa."

Linna stiffened. Things were still not going well with Papa. She just couldn't forgive him for not telling them the truth about the home they were moving to in Canada. Then, all the stories Mama told Papa about the homeland last night made Linna sad and more homesick than ever. Finally, she'd covered her head with the scratchy blanket and held her hands over her ears to block out their voices. She'd fallen asleep with tears streaming from her eyes and her sobs muffled against the pillow.

To change the subject she asked, "How long have you been in Canada?"

Kat joined her on the path. "This is my third summer."

"Really?" Linna said, staring at Kat. "Have you lived in a soddie all this time?"

Kat shrugged. "Yes. It's not so bad. We have many friends here."

The path led past the end of the whitewashed houses to a small wooden box, about a metre square, plopped on the ground. Linna gazed around, looking for the stream or river, but there wasn't one.

The sight of a wooden pump handle sticking out of the box brought tears to Linna's eyes, as she realized the water must be in the ground. She missed the Atmühl River that had flowed through the village, and past Colmberg Castle. In Germany there was always plenty of crystal clear water. Here, like everything else they needed, it seemed water came out of the dark earth.

Linna gulped. More than anything she wanted Kat to like her, so she didn't want to argue about soddies. Every day for nearly five years she and Elli had played together, worked together, gone to school together. Leaving her behind had been terrible. Linna finally asked, "Is it difficult to get the water?"

Kat stepped up to the pump, setting her bucket under the spout. "Not really, except the well is nearly dry. We can only get a few pails at a time, then nothing comes."

She pumped the handle: screech-squawk. Up and down it went, but nothing came out.

"Is it empty now?" Linna asked. Perhaps it just took the water a long time to come from wherever it was beneath the ground.

Kat didn't answer.

In a few seconds, water gushed down the spout, splashing into the pail on the wooden platform. Kat continued to pump. "When my pail is full pull it out and stick yours in. I'll keep pumping so the water stays coming."

Quick to comply, Linna dragged it aside and slipped the empty one into place. Cold water splattered her arms and chest, making big wet blotches on the front of her everyday navy blue dress. "Brrr," she said, laughing as she thought of herself as a little dog taking its first leap into the river in spring. Maybe she should shake the water off. "It's funny the water is so cold when it's hot outside."

"Under the ground it's always cold in the summertime, but warmer in the winter, otherwise it would freeze over like the water pail," said Kat. "Soddies are like that too." She pumped the handle a few more times before stopping. The pail filled slowly from the water still trickling out of the spout.

Linna grabbed her pail, feeling the weight stretch her arm as if it could grow long enough to let the bucket settle back onto the ground.

Kat picked up her pail and trudged ahead, not seeming to mind the weight.

"You're very strong," Linna said, envying her strength. "I bet you're younger than me and I can hardly lift it."

"I'm eleven. But I'll turn twelve on the first day of November. I always haul the water unless it's winter and we can melt snow, then I bring it in instead."

Linna shifted the pail to in front of herself, gripping the metal handle with both of her hands. With each step more water slopped over the edges, soaking quickly into the path. At home in Germany there'd been uncles and aunts and grown cousins all near Nana's house, so she'd never had to carry a pail full of water before. She said, "I was twelve on March eighth, so I am older than you."

Kat turned back and smiled. "After you carry lots of pails of water you'll be stronger than me, I bet. Wait until washday."

Linna hadn't thought of that! Goodness how would they get enough water to wash their clothes without a river, especially since there was so much dust in this country? It had been difficult on the long trip over the ocean, but this was forever. Last night when she had washed her face after so many days without water except to drink on the train, it had felt so good. Water on the train had cost so much they had to make what they brought last the whole trip.

"I suppose I will get stronger," she said hopefully, setting the pail down in front of herself, although she didn't really believe it.

Kat stopped, setting hers down too. "You need to carry it with one hand first, holding it out, then stop and switch hands." She opened her hand to reveal the red line that marked where she'd been gripping the bucket.

Linna tried again, taking a deep breath. She imagined the pail was full of sweet-smelling flowers she and Elli had picked from the rolling green German hillsides, and she was taking them home for Mama. It helped.

Before long Kat stopped in front of a large soddie. "This is where I live. Do you want to play after I'm done my chores? Maybe we can go to the races together?"

"Races?" asked Linna, setting her pail on the ground.

"Oh yes, it's Canada's birthday today. She's forty-three years old and there is a celebration in Qu'Appelle. All the stores will be closed for a half-day and the Sports Club has horse races. They're very grand. Some men play the bagpipes and everyone picks their favourite horse."

"Papa didn't mention anything," said Linna. To be truthful though, she hadn't been listening, so she might just not have heard. "I've never been to real horse races, but Papa wrote us letters about them. At home the big horse race is at Oktoberfest in Ansbach, and we never went."

Linna remembered one of Papa's letters giving exciting descriptions of the horses galloping along the prairie track, and the crowd cheering them. He'd even mentioned the strange sound of the bagpipes and the men in skirts who played them. She giggled. "Do grown men truly wear skirts to play these bagpipes?"

"They're called kilts," said Kat, "and they do. At first I put my hands over my ears when I heard bagpipes, since they're not like the horns my uncles played. But after awhile I decided they sounded fine."

Even though she wasn't really sure she wanted to celebrate the birthday of this hot, ugly country, Linna wanted more than anything to make friends. "I'll ask if I can go with you," she said. Besides, if she went with Kat, then she wouldn't have to go with Papa.

Kat grinned. "I'll come to your house right after I finish my chores."

Linna waited until Kat disappeared inside before hoisting her pail again. Even though the grasshoppers still hopped between the soddies, the sun still burned down on her head, and the puffs of wind still made her even hotter, she felt better. A few random words from *Tristan und Isolde* floated through her memory, *Mir erkoren, mir verloren.* She began to sing, "Chosen to be mine, lost to me." It was, she felt, like the words were truly hers now, with Germany her homeland on the other side of the world. When she couldn't hit Isolde's high notes, she switched to a *lieder,* the kind of song Tante Karoline told her opera singers sang to train their voices, and performed at recitals. Carefully shaping her mouth to the sounds, she began one of Strauss's songs, *"Nennen sol ich sagt ihr."*

The song somehow lightened her load, so the pail was not nearly such a heavy chore as she trudged the remaining distance. She opened the door to the soddie, determined to convince Mama to let her go with Kat. Surprisingly, she agreed right away. She said they were supposed to meet papa at the fairgrounds after work – it was a surprise for Konrad and Linna. But she was pleased Linna had already made a friend. So after munching down a quick meal of radishes on bread for her lunch, Linna hurried away with Kat.

The road into town was dusty. Overhead a few puffy clouds floated over the sun once in awhile, providing momentary shade from the burning rays. Linna and Kat moved over several times as they heard the clip-clop of horses' hooves coming up behind them. Some of them pulled fancy black buggies, with two people nestled under a canopy from the sun, while others dragged worn, rattling wagons. The dust that followed them choked Linna and made her sneeze.

"I wish I could ride in a buggy," Kat said. "I bet it's smoother than the wagon Papa borrows from the mill."

Linna nodded, realizing it must be the same one her papa had used yesterday. "Me too. But I'd like to ride in a motorcar even more. I saw some of them in Halifax at the Immigration Centre while we were there."

"Oh yes! There are a few cars in town. It would be nice to have one of those. Or even a bicycle. Lots of children have them."

"Really?" Linna said. "Not me. I don't think I would be able to keep it upright."

Kat giggled. "I saw Sarah Booker crash hers in the spring. She toppled right into the mud with her fancy dress, then screamed at all of us to go away. She wasn't allowed to play outside the rest of the week and missed all of the fun."

"Who is Sarah Booker?"

"A girl who doesn't like me. I don't think she likes anyone from south of the train tracks."

Linna remembered the girl from the station. "Does she have blonde hair, just like her father's, and a fancy carriage to ride in?"

"Yes," Kat said. "Her family's been here since the town became Qu'Appelle Station in 1884. The Duke of Hartington is her great-uncle, or so she tells us all the time. You'd think that mattered to everyone in Canada. But her mother did inherit lots of money when some relative died awhile ago."

"She said I was a..." Linna concentrated for a moment to recall the strange English word, "...a squatter. What does that mean?"

Kat groaned. "Squatters are people who don't own their land. The CPR, who are the railroad company, own our land. Our homes are all just built there and they've never made us leave."

"Isn't that stealing?" Linna asked, feeling even angrier with Papa.

"Papa says they don't use the land for anything, and they don't mind us staying here. It's not like they can't see our homes."

Before Linna could respond, a boy galloping past on a tall bay horse distracted her. The horse's black mane and tail rippled in the breeze, while the rider seemed glued to the big leather saddle. He reminded her of the fox hunts held at Colmberg Castle whenever there were guests staying. For the past year Tante Karoline had taken her and Elli to help in the kitchen each time there were visitors, so she had seen many interesting things.

Kat nodded at the passing rider. "I bet he's racing this afternoon. He comes to school every day on his horse."

While Linna had been interested in the racing before, seeing the boy made excitement surge through her. She had thought it was something only grown-ups did and children watched. It would be even more fun with young people competing. "How many races are there?"

"Depends how many people bring their horses to race."

"Let's hurry." Linna quickened her pace. A bird, hidden in a half-grown tree, erupted into a song that filled her heart. "Will you show me everything?"

"Of course."

Linna picked her way over the steel rails and big black railroad ties of the tracks, after checking to make sure there wasn't a train in sight. The train ride seemed much longer ago than yesterday.

She passed the mill, careful to look out at the field of grain instead. Mama had told her that Papa was supposed to work until one o'clock, and then meet them at the fair.

"See that house? That's where Sarah lives," Kat said, pointing to a white house with a veranda all the way around the front.

It had taken Linna a while to get used to seeing verandas on the fanciest houses as the train rolled through towns. She had never seen one in Germany. A lady had told her it was so the family could sit outside in the evening, instead of inside in the heat. But Germany was never as hot as Canada, so houses there hadn't needed them. Linna sighed. Sarah's family were truly rich to have such a grand home. It was one of the nicest in the town. "I wish we could live in a house like that," she said.

"Her family owns the farmland on the other side of the road, so that big red barn is theirs too. But they live on the town side."

"Oh," said Linna, thinking how different she would feel if she wasn't a squatter, but lived in the town. Perhaps someday Papa would have enough money for a real house.

Further along the street a lady and three small children made their way to the fairgrounds. A man leaning on a cane opened the gate of his yard, and beamed at Kat as they passed.

"Hello, hello, Katarine," called the rosy-cheeked woman who followed him out. Behind her a vine covered the front of the tiny house. Flowers of rich gold and orange bloomed alongside the front steps.

"Hello, Mrs. Lazurko," Kat replied. "Are you going to the horse races?"

The woman nodded. "Of course. We have to celebrate Canada's birthday." Her English words had a strong accent.

"Where's Pauline?"

Shaking her head, Mrs. Lazurko said, "Ah, that girl, she's always in a hurry. She's been gone for an hour already."

"Thanks! See you later." Kat waved as they resumed their walk. "Pauline's in the grade below me. She's lucky – she was born in Canada. Mrs. Lazurko tells great stories about how she came from the Ukraine to marry Mr. Lazurko in 1898, even though she'd never met him. She says he was a nice surprise."

"What happened to his leg?"

"He works in the livery stable and a horse kicked him. His leg was broken, and it's still weak," answered Kat.

The fairgrounds lay beyond the last neat block of houses, and looked like empty prairie except for the row of spectator stands and a single long, low building. Linna guessed there were already a few hundred people walking around or climbing into the stands. But the most exciting thing she saw was the dozens of horses at the far side of the field.

"Let's hurry," Linna said, quickening her pace. "It looks like there's lots going on."

"Where do you want to watch from?"

Linna shrugged, deciding it was wiser to let her new friend's experience guide them. "I don't know. You choose."

Taking long strides, Kat walked across the grassy grounds. Half a dozen horses stood in the shade of a small poplar bluff, their tails switching back and forth to brush the flies off their backs. Men gathered in small groups, some standing and holding their horses' reins, while others leaned back in the comfort of their saddles, talking to one another.

"I like to be near the finish line," Kat said. "Then you can see the winners. Do you want some water first?"

Water sounded like a good idea to Linna. She was glad she'd borrowed the light blue cotton bonnet Kat offered. Even with it protecting her head from the sun, she felt a little dizzy. She nodded at Kat. "Please."

A dozen or more people hovered around the long building with the open front. "The ladies from all the churches bring things to drink and eat," Kat said. "Most of it you have to buy, but sometimes they give children cold tea with lemon. Do you want to check?"

"Sure," said Linna, hurrying behind Kat.

Rows of pies lined the front counter: pies piled high with brown-tipped swirls of meringue, pies with perfect little squares in the top crust so the filling peeped through, and pies sprinkled with cinnamon and sugar. Linna ran her tongue over her lips, tasting one in her imagination. She wished she had pennies in her pocket to buy a piece.

People shuffled around Linna. Their words were difficult for her to understand as she only heard fragments of conversations. A heavy man, his rotund tummy touching the counter, let out a big belly laugh that made everyone turn to stare. Immediately, a lady whose long thin face was scrunched into a grimace, nudged him in the ribs with her elbow.

"You shouldn't even be looking at those pies because I know you have no money," warned a voice beside Linna.

She felt herself go limp. Before she turned, Linna knew there was only one person who could be speaking. She looked into Sarah Booker's deep blue eyes. "Well, umm..." she mumbled, not sure how to answer, as she stared enviously at Sarah's crisp yellow cotton dress. Her own clothes were already wrinkled and dusty.

"We didn't touch anything," Kat said, arching her shoulders. "We can look if we want."

Sarah continued, ignoring the explanation, "If you touch one single thing I'll tell my mother."

Too embarrassed to answer, Linna kept her eyes focused on the ladies hustling around inside the little building. Sure enough, the lady who had ridden away yesterday with Sarah picked up one of the pies to serve a young man. The smile on her face seemed friendly but distant, all at the same time.

Linna whispered to Kat, "Let's just go. Water is good for me."

"Don't be mean Sarah," said a red-headed boy, stepping forward. His face under his flat black cap was flushed pink around his freckles, like he didn't often spend time outdoors. "Everyone can look. Hello, Kat."

"Hello, Henry," Kat said. "This is my friend Linna. She lives near me."

Sarah ignored the introductions, turned to Henry and said, "You can't tell me what to do, Henry Spencer. I'll be with Eunice, if you want to watch the races with us." She walked into the crowd without waiting for a reply.

"Hello, Linna." Henry smiled, then turned back to Kat and said, "Maybe you did want to stick your finger in one of those pies! They sure look good."

"Don't tease," said Kat, laughing. "We're just looking for something to drink."

"My mother is giving children free cups of tea if you'd like," Henry said.

"Sure. Just move further down, Linna," Kat directed. "Stop in front of the lady with the grey dress."

Doing as she was told, Linna moved away from the tempting pies. She felt even dizzier than before, and was thankful Henry had arrived.

"Are you feeling all right, Henry?" said the lady holding a big ladle. "Would you girls like some cold tea? It's free for children today."

Henry nodded, but didn't answer.

"Yes, thank you," Kat said. "It's very hot, isn't it?"

Linna reached out thankfully to accept the cup of tea, which she drank in two big gulps. Kat was just as fast. Then, following Kat's lead, she handed the tin cup back to the lady, who dropped them into a big wash pan behind her.

When Linna looked around again Henry had also disappeared. Perhaps, she decided, he'd gone to join Sarah.

The crowd behind Linna had doubled while they stood in line, and the friendly chatter grew even louder and harder to understand. She wished she could put her hands over her ears and block some of it out.

"Follow me," Kat said, leading her away past the grandstands, towards a stake that marked the end of the race course. "It'll be starting soon."

Linna flopped on the ground, ready to rest for a few minutes. The grass was crackly underneath her, poking her right through the thin fabric of her dress. She fanned her face with her hand, wondering how long it would take her to become as used to the heat as Kat seemed to be. Only a dozen or so people stood nearby, their words thankfully lost on the breeze, with most of the spectators filling the grandstands or lining up at the starting line.

"That Sarah is so uppity," said Kat, dropping onto the ground beside Linna. "Just talk right back to her, so she doesn't think she can boss you around."

While it sounded like good advice, Linna wasn't sure she could follow it. Maybe if she wasn't really a squatter, or had some money, or could speak English better, she'd feel braver. Everything about Sarah made her feel nervous. But she'd try: if Kat could do it, maybe she could too.

Three men in colourful skirts strode up to the starting line, their hairy legs and knobbly knees visible to everyone. Linna clapped her hand over her mouth to hold back laughter. She was glad Papa hadn't moved to Scotland, where they came from! Perhaps everyone wore skirts there. A tall man, dressed in a black suit and wearing a great top hat stood beside them, speaking. Linna wished she were closer, to hear the words.

"It's the starting ceremony," Kat said. "Soon you'll hear the bagpipes. The first thing they play is always "The Maple Leaf," especially today for Canada's birthday. At the end we sing "God Save the King," even though he died in the spring."

Linna watched as the men straightened and prepared to blow. The powerful sounds still took her by surprise. Clamping both hands over her ears, she listened to the bellowing that made her think of a giant animal in pain.

But as the pipers continued to play, a chill went through her, even though the heat was exactly the same as it had been. It felt like the music could rattle her bones. While it didn't make her want to sing, she soon dropped her hands, listening with fascination.

"See," Kat said. "I told you it wasn't bad after you got used to it."

Linna smiled. "Yes, but it sure was a surprise in the first minute!"

The bagpipe players soon finished, then made way for the race to begin. Eight horses moved forward to line up in an almost-straight row, with space between them. It wasn't, as Linna had expected, orderly at all. The animals bumped and whinnied, lunging backwards and forwards. A tall red roan reared, nearly dumping its rider on the ground. When its feet hit the dirt again, it was ahead of the others, so had to back into place.

"That's Red Pepper," Kat said, pointing. "He runs every time and wins lots of races."

"It's a good name. He looks speckled with red pepper and salt." As the seconds passed Adeline was hardly able to catch her breath, as if it was waiting at the start line, too.

The man in the top hat stood on the sidelines, his pistol pointed in the air. Finally Red Pepper was still. Boom! The starter's shot rang out over the fairgrounds.

It seemed exactly the same instant when all of the horses bolted forward, their bodies stretched out. With each stride their long legs hurtled ahead and their hooves pounded the ground. Linna's body tingled with excitement. She felt for a second like she was flying on one of them.

"Go, Red Pepper, go!" shouted Kat beside her.

The grounds filled with a chorus of screams and cheers, as everyone yelled the name of their favourite horse.

Red Pepper leapt to the front of the pack. His rider leaned forward in the saddle, hunched like a cat about to pounce.

The halfway point! The boy they'd seen on the bay inched his way up to Red Pepper's tail.

A woman to Linna's right shouted hysterically. But Linna kept her eyes riveted on the race.

"Here they come!" Kat's words flew out in excited little gasps. "See the red flag? That's the other side of the finish line."

A second passed.

The thunder of hooves echoed. The crowd screamed, yelled, shook their arms, and cheered, as all eight horses neared the end of the track.

Red Pepper led by a head. A palomino was up to his shoulders, with the bay now a nose behind.

"Go, Red Pepper, go!" screamed Kat, jumping up and down, and waving her arms.

Without really deciding who she wanted to win, Linna cheered as well. "*Schnell!* Faster!" Maybe the palomino coming from behind would take one longer stride and pull past Red Pepper. Or perhaps the boy on the bay would win.

The rider on the palomino leaned further ahead. He urged the animal forward.

Beside him, Red Pepper stretched out full-length. He was close enough to Linna that she could see his nostrils flare as he put all his strength into the last stride.

She made up her mind. "Go Red Pepper, go!"

Linna kept her eyes on the red flag; afraid she'd miss the instant of victory.

Red Pepper made a giant leap, taking the win! Elation filled her.

Then she caught sight of Sarah cheering wildly on the opposite side of the track. A little of the thrill of celebrating Canada's birthday disappeared.

CHAPTER 3

Linna bounced on Mama's bed, waiting impatiently for Kat to arrive. She stared at the pages and pages of newspapers tacked to the walls, and felt embarrassed, even though it was nice to see something besides black dirt inside. Surely, families in real houses in Canada used real wallpaper like they sold in stores, not newspaper, to cover their walls.

Two days ago, Mama and Anke had dragged everything out of the soddie, except for the big stove, and began with the pile of old newspapers Anke brought for them. They'd even found an old tarpaulin the mill foreman had thrown out, that had just a few holes, to tack up to the ceiling to keep the dirt from falling in Linna's eyes while she slept. While it still wasn't beautiful, it did make the room less ugly.

"Now it's as nice on the inside, as the outside," Anke had said. "Your soddie is done."

"*Danke,* thank you," Mama had answered, working on her new English words with Anke's help.

With the family's treasures from Germany spread out, it looked almost like home. A nice white cloth with Mama's embroidery work covered the tiny table. The picture that cousin Wilhelm had painted of Nana's cottage hung on the long wall over the big bed. Linna was glad he'd made it as a gift for them, so her memories of Germany would never fade.

Even Linna had a tiny shelf on the wall now, to keep her treasures. The doll Nana had made her when she was five sat stiffly on one side, like it was disappointed not to be a plaything anymore. With its dress of white puffy sleeves, red-checked dirndl skirt and red apron, the doll made Linna homesick. Beside it, her tiny hand-painted china teacup and saucer, which Tante Karoline had given as a parting gift, sat safely away from Konrad's busy fingers.

"Why won't you come outside and play with me?" Konrad said, nodding toward the door. "I want to throw horseshoes. I can even hit the peg "

"Only if you stand beside it," said Linna. She had already taken Konrad with her on four trips to the well, letting him pump the handle up and down twenty times before the water ran. While it was fun to teach him new things, she was ready to spend time with her friend.

Konrad backed up to the far corner. "Oh no! I can stand back this far and still hit it. I beat Dieter every time."

"Maybe tomorrow. Go practise with Dieter now. But you're too little for horseshoes anyway," Linna said. "The men play that game."

Indeed, Papa and many of the other men in their little community often played at night, taking turns tossing worn steel horseshoes at a stake in the ground. Linna didn't really have to try to avoid Papa at all; it seemed he was either at the mill, or doing books for someone, or else spending the coolness of the evening outdoors. It had been a terrible surprise to learn he spent one night every week doing accounts for the Bookers. While Linna knew it was the only way they could ever hope to have a house in town, or for Papa to get a job in banking again, she still wished he could work for someone else.

"Yes," Mama said, coming in the door, "you should go outside to play now before it gets too hot. The ground has nearly dried up from the little bit of rain that fell." She dropped the corners she was holding on her apron, emptying it of the small pile of vegetables she'd gathered.

"There's not much ready yet, is there?" Linna asked. Each day Mama picked what she could, but they still had to buy most things from the store.

"No," Mama said shortly. "It will be good if you and Kat find some wild berries to pick. Tomorrow you can show me, if there are lots. There is too little rain for a good garden."

Linna pulled on her bonnet strings, anxious for Kat to arrive before Mama decided she had to take Konrad with her. "I'll take these syrup pails with me to bring back what I find, all right?"

Mama gave her a quick hug. "That will be fine. *Danke*. Have a nice walk."

Linna slipped out the door just as Kat arrived. "Hello. Can we go now?"

"Yes," Kat said, swinging two small pails just like Linna's. "But Mama says we must be back by early afternoon. She's worried about the weather."

"It seems fine to me." Linna looked up, shielding her eyes from the hot sun working its way across the sky. She stared at Kat's bare feet, wondering for the hundredth time how anyone could stand to walk through the prickly dry grass and thistles without shoes. Linna had tried, but soon put them back on.

The morning was cooler after the rain, although inside the soddie's thick walls Linna hadn't heard a thing in the night. There had been, however, enough rain to wash the dust from things, making the day seem fresh and clean, and her heart lighter with it.

Linna walked next to Kat, telling her all about the area she came from in Germany, and Colmberg Castle. Kat barely remembered the old country, since she was only eight when her family left.

"What was the best thing that ever happened in the castle?" Kat asked.

"Seeing Gisela Staudigl," answered Linna quickly. "Tante Karoline took Elli and me to help carry food to the great hall for the dinner, and wash up dishes afterwards, of course. But she let me sneak in behind the door and listen to her sing the part of Brangäne from *Tristan und Isolde.* Her voice lifted higher and higher, until it sounded like she sang from heaven itself with the angels."

Linna thought about telling Kat that she wanted to sing opera too, but kept still. It seemed too lofty a dream for someone who lived in a soddie.

As they walked, not speaking, there was a steady rustling of grasshoppers moving through the prairie, their bodies browner now, like the grass, instead of green. Linna had grown used to them, and just shook her arm when one landed on her, sending it flying. Finally she asked, "How do you know where we are? It all looks the same to me."

"We're going south, towards the sun. We follow this road for a long ways. There are farms along the way so we can't get lost. See up there – that stone house. Isn't it beautiful? I'd like a stone house."

Linna squinted into the bright sunshine, trying to make out its features. It was tall, with long, narrow windows, and stood alone on the crest of a hill, like a prairie castle.

"Wouldn't it be hard to find so many stones?" Linna asked with surprise. She hadn't noticed many rocks at all in Qu'Appelle, just pebbles that pushed through the soles of her worn shoes.

"In town it would, but out here some of the farms have lots of big stones."

Gazing at the nearby crop Linna realized it was true. The sparse stalks of grain had rocks scattered here and there between them. "For my house, I'd like anything but sod," she said.

Overhead the sky was clear, all traces of the morning's clouds vanished like Nana's *Kartoffelsalat mit Hering,* potato salad with herring. In the past few days Linna had hungered for a taste of fish in this waterless land.

"Here, we'll head east now," said Kat. "See, there's a good path to follow. We're going to my favourite spot."

"What made the path?" Linna said, realizing this one didn't have the double grooves of wagon ruts she'd grown used to. "An animal?"

"Cows or maybe deer, grazing around this bush."

At least some things were the same in Canada as in Germany: the deer ran wild through the land here too and Anke often brought them venison to cook. So did rabbits and hare. Linna could almost imagine herself back to the old country when one hopped past.

Protruding from the grass, not far from the path, was an enormous white rock so big it looked like a cow lying down, half buried in dirt. Further on, the path dipped into the trees, so the poplars shaded Linna from the sun. A wild rose, its prickly thorns protecting the full bloom, rubbed against her leg. She stopped and glanced down to see if her skin was scratched.

Kat asked, "Are you okay?"

"Yes." Linna gazed across the slight roll of the prairie ahead, wondering what there could possibly be to pick there besides grass.

Kat pointed to a spot ahead and began to run. "Wild strawberries! They're so good. Let's eat some now."

Linna moved slowly, not understanding what Kat could be talking about. "But strawberries grow in forests and shaded places."

"Not in Canada." Kat grinned, flopped onto the ground, and popped several berries into her mouth. "Here they grow in the bright sunlight."

Linna dropped to her knees. At first she saw nothing but the reddish runners of the strawberry plants tangled in the grass, but then she spied a tiny berry under a jagged green leaf. Her fingers clamped around the soft warm berry, which was only the size of the nail on her little finger. But when the sweetness of it melted against her tongue, she knew why Kat had been so excited to find them.

After the snack Kat set off at a brisk pace, walking for a while before she said, "Do you like it? This is my favourite spot."

The tallest, sturdiest tree Linna had seen on the prairies stood alone in the middle of a low grassy paddock, a distance away from a circle of poplars. "What kind of tree is that?" she asked.

"A cottonwood, I think – in the spring the ground around it is covered with its white fuzzy seeds."

Dots of colour spread throughout the grass too, reminding Linna of the flower gardens around the castle grounds. She dropped down against the smooth bark of the old tree, enjoying the shade its full branches and triangular-shaped leaves provided. Overhead a bluebird chirped at her invasion.

Kat dropped to the ground beside her. "I come here to think; it's so peaceful. Of course our house is noisy with my three little brothers."

Linna wondered how Kat's whole family lived in a single room, but she didn't like to ask too many questions. "One brother is enough for me."

"What is your very favourite thing?" Kat said. "Mine is taking apart the worn clothes and using the different-shaped parts to make pictures for a quilt cover. I can only use the cloth that isn't thin, so I have to fit all the pieces together until they look like something. I help Mama make rag rugs out of the worn parts that are left over."

"That sounds pretty," Linna said. "Will you show me one when we get back?" She didn't enjoy the time she spent learning needlework at all, but she was glad Kat did. From the amount of time Mama worked at her sewing, she guessed she would have to learn to like it sooner or later.

"Yes. But what do you like to do best?"

Of course Linna knew what she loved most. But she couldn't imagine the dream ever happening anymore. It was Papa's dream they were following in Canada, not hers. "Singing," she said with a sigh, not even including the opera part.

"Singing? Oh let me hear you!"

Getting up, Linna left her tin pails on the ground beside the plants. She stood straight, staring out across the prairie, then began to turn, ever so slowly, like the second hand on Papa's pocket watch. Here and there poplar trees marked the hours, while golden sunflowers and purple blazingstars and orange wood lilies kept the minutes.

A happy smile sprang to Linna's face as she turned to face Kat again. She opened her mouth, and began to sing one of her favourite hymns.

> *"Dear Christians, one and all, rejoice,*
> *With exultation springing,*
> *And, with united heart and voice,*
> *And holy rapture singing,*
> *Proclaim the wonders God hath done."*

"Oh, that's beautiful," exclaimed Kat. "You have such a pretty voice."

"Thank you," whispered Linna. A flood of feelings she couldn't talk about filled her. Today she could see the wonders of the prairie, so maybe if she tried harder she would like it here.

"Do you want to climb the tree?" asked Kat, seeming to understand Linna's quiet moment. "You can see a long ways from the top branches."

Linna pulled herself up by the lowest solid limb, using her shoes to awkwardly grip the tree. Above her Kat shot to the top, her bare feet clinging to the bark like fingers to sticky pull taffy!

Tired with her exertion in the heat, Linna panted as she settled on a branch and finally looked out at the surrounding country. Kat was right: she could see forever. "Can this be *my* favourite place, too?" she asked.

"Sure." Kat ran her hand through the long curls she had tied back with a piece of blue yarn. "You're my very best friend and I will share everything with you. Before you came there were no other German girls my age, just boys."

"You're my best friend, too," said Linna, thankful to have a friend. Yesterday she had written Elli a long letter, telling her all about Kat and Canada. All the good things; she'd left out the details of the soddie, so Elli wouldn't worry about her.

Kat wiggled above her, making the leaves dance. "We'd better gather some things and start back, before the bad weather comes."

Going down was easier than up. Linna dropped the last bit to the ground, landing with a thud.

Kat led the way again. "There are some nice tall pigweeds here. They'll be good."

"Pigweed? What an awful name for food." Linna stared at the tall, spindly green plants with the narrow, almost silverish leaves.

Snapping them off at the stem, Kat quickly picked a pailful. "Sarah Booker's mother says they're Lambs Quarters. She doesn't like the name pigweed either."

"Sarah's mother cooks these?" said Linna in surprise.

"Only in the spring, because they're the first green plants to grow. She tells everyone she's planted them in her garden and she doesn't cook the ones that grow wild around her house. Oh, and there's also dandelions that come early." Kat blew at the white fluff covering a withered dandelion plant, spreading the seeds across the grass. "You have to boil dandelions when they're old like this, and they don't taste as good as salad."

Linna followed Kat's lead, picking as many as she could push into one of her pails. "Anke can probably tell Mama what to do with them."

Kat nodded. "There aren't many left around town anymore, because we eat so many when they're fresh in the spring. They taste so good after a long winter with nothing green to eat."

As they made their way back Linna recognized landmarks along the trail. Feeling proud of herself, she hummed a little more of her favourite hymn.

"Do you smell that?" asked Kat.

Linna sniffed. "Well, I smell something, but I'm not sure what it is."

"Mint. Mama says it's a different kind than in Germany, but it's very nice for tea."

Pleased to find a treat for Mama, Linna walked into the low marshy dip behind Kat. "Oh no, it's wet!"

"You wait," said Kat, "I'll bring some back for you. This is usually a slough, but this year it's almost dried up." A duck, still paddling in the small pool of water at its centre suddenly squawked, flapped its wings and headed skyward.

In a minute Kat returned, her feet dark with mud socks. She stretched one foot out in front of her, wiggling her toes.

"Thank you," Linna said, adding the strong-smelling, soft green leaves to the top of her pail. Mama had been very quiet these past few days, so maybe this would cheer her up. At night she and Papa whispered for a long while before they fell asleep, and sometimes her voice grew loud like they were arguing.

Kat wiped her feet back and forth across the grass, smearing the mud streaks. "They look almost like Sarah's fancy shoes, don't you think, with the ankle straps?"

Linna grinned, imaging the fastidious Sarah mucking about like Kat. "I can't even imagine Sarah wiping mud off those shoes, never mind being barefoot in it."

"You're right," Kat said. "Her mother would never let her. Guess we'd better go."

Before long they came to a bluff, where Kat said, "Let's see if there are some early ripe Saskatoon berries. In a few weeks we'll be able to pick them to sell to the ladies in town. Then raspberries and chokecherries after that."

"Really?" Linna felt a surge of excitement staring at the trees. She had never thought about earning money of her own in Canada. "How much could I get?"

"As much as a ten-cent piece for each pail. I'll take you to the houses that pay the best."

At last something good seemed possible. An idea suddenly filled Linna's head and heart. Maybe she could earn enough money to return home to Germany, if not forever, at least until Papa built a house for them.

Kat yanked a few purplish berries off a tree that wasn't much higher than her shoulders, and handed them to Linna. "Taste them. Saskatoon berries are even better than Canadian strawberries."

Saskatoon berries were small, perfect little balls about one centimetre wide, with the dried-up brown bits of their flowers on the ends. Linna dropped one into her mouth, squishing the juice out between her teeth and feeling the tiny seeds poke her tongue. She smiled at Kat. "They are good! No wonder people will pay so much for them."

"You should taste a Saskatoon pie," Kat said, leaning further into the tree to find more purple berries among the red ones.

Searching for the few ripe ones, Linna worked her way deeper into the bush. She climbed over broken branches. She dropped down to sit on spindly broken-off tree trunks not much thicker than the branches. She climbed onto a dirt clump to reach for a nearly purple Saskatoon berry.

"Move!" Kat yelled.

Linna jumped. "What's wrong? Where should I go?" She couldn't see anything to be afraid of: no wild animals or poison ivy plants.

"Don't you feel them? Look at your legs!" squealed Kat.

Linna looked down. Half a dozen tiny red dots raced up her stockings. She screamed, nearly spilling her berry pail.

Kat rushed up and yanked Linna's arm to pull her away from the mound she stood on. "See? That's a red ant pile."

"I feel one biting," Linna yelled. The bite stung worse than anything she had ever felt. "Get it off me! Get it off!"

Kat set her pail down, and ran both of her hands down Linna's legs, squashing the wiggly red ants. Digging her fingers deep into the soft moist soil around the bottom of the bushes, she brought up a handful, which she smeared on the welts appearing on Linna's legs.

"They sting!" Linna cried. Her eyes filled with tears, and she felt like clawing at the welts to tear them from her skin.

"Of course. Red ants bite, but the dirt will take the sting away in a few minutes. Sit on the ground."

Linna dropped obediently, leaned against a small poplar, and stared at the crumbling soil that had already started to fall off her legs. Surprisingly, the pain began to subside.

"Hold the moist dirt over the ones that sting the worst," Kat said, digging for a fresh handful.

They pressed the cold dirt onto the welts for a few minutes, until the pain was no more than that of pin poking her while Mama was fitting a new dress. Linna said, "It's all right now. None of them hurt too much."

"Good." Kat stared at Linna's legs. "Now we're twins, only you have dirty brown legs and I have dirty brown feet."

Linna couldn't smile at the joke, instead she wished she could cry. It seemed strange that dirt was used for everything in Canada. "Thank you. I'm glad you were here. I didn't know dirt would help a bite."

"You're welcome. Let's go and pick our strawberries to take home." Kat grabbed Linna's pails, and handed them to her before she retrieved her own.

Squatting between the runners of plants in the strawberry patch, it occurred to Linna that she didn't feel like she'd just opened the oven door of Mama's new stove anymore. She peered up at the sky, where a thick dark cloud floated over the sun. "Kat, maybe your Mama was right." She pointed at the clouds.

"Mama's always right about the weather. We'd better hurry."

Linna grabbed both of her pails and set off behind Kat. She didn't want to rush, or the berries would squish in the pail, turning to mush. But she kept a nervous watch on the sky as more clouds appeared, each one darker than the last.

"Have you ever been out in a storm?" Linna took a long stride beside Kat, careful not to let their pails bump together.

"Not really," said Kat, her voice small. "Mama always makes us come in before the weather gets bad. One of her brothers was hit by lightning as a child, so she's very scared."

"Oh." Tante Karoline had talked about severe thunderstorms in the Alps, where she'd gone as a maid with the Baroness once, but they were not common where Nana lived, far away from the mountains.

"The first summer we were in Canada it thunderstormed nearly every night. Mama had a very bad time. This year there haven't been many, so she's happy."

Linna decided she knew how Kat's mama felt, as her stomach twisted with knots. She watched the bright streaks of lightning on the horizon, knowing they were moving closer. If she strained her ears she heard the lowest rumblings of thunder echo after each bolt.

The breeze, which had felt hot against her skin just half an hour ago, suddenly seemed ice-cold. In a few seconds it changed from gently rustling the leaves in the trees, to a monster that ripped branches and hurled them across the fields. Fear rose in Linna, as she gave up trying to keep the berries from shaking, and began to run with Kat along the trail.

A crop beside the edge of the path leaned in the wind, as though an invisible person was lying on it, pushing it to the ground. Dirt from a plowed field lifted and flew, filling the air with grit. Since both of her hands were full, Linna couldn't even rub her eyes to try to clear them. Instead she faced into the wind, fighting to make each step as her dress flattened against her body.

Kat stopped, staring up at the sky. "Look!" she cried with horror, "It's a funnel cloud!"

Turning her back to the wind, Linna searched the dark clouds. There it was! The sky was alive with a whirling, twirling mass of charcoal grey clouds that had a greenish tinge, out of which dropped a narrow tip — the funnel of a cyclone.

"Do they happen here often?" Linna asked, her shout sounding like a whisper in the wind. She'd only heard of one ever happening in Mama or Papa's lifetime at home.

"Yes. There were three last summer, but none touched down near us."

Linna stood mesmerized by the sight. The wind stole her breath and dirt pelted her body. Clouds spun, bringing the funnel closer and closer.

The cyclone seemed headed for the very spot where she stood.

"Run!" Kat yelled, her voice a shriek of terror. "We'll crouch down beside the big rock - in that low spot out of the wind. Maybe it will miss us if it touches down."

Linna had to save herself. She pivoted and found the huge white rock she'd noticed earlier. It was half buried. Nothing could pull it out of the ground. Racing behind Kat, she covered the distance in a few seconds.

Boom! Boom!

Completely out of breath, Linna dropped down with her back to the boulder. Goosebumps covered her arms from the cold wind and fear. The terrible roar filled her head like a nightmare she couldn't wake up from. She closed her eyes, but she couldn't close her ears.

Kat's face was white as she set down her pails, rose up on her knees, and turned to watch the oncoming storm. Linna guessed her face probably looked the same.

The sound was worse than a freight train rolling right beside them.

"It's touching down!" Kat screamed. She huddled below the edge of the rock, gripping Linna's hand so hard it ached. "We have to lie flat on the ground."

Linna threw herself down on the grass, their hands still clenched together. A thorny thistle scratched her ankle. Purple locoweed tickled her nose, overwhelming her with its perfume. She felt the cyclone coming — closer and closer - until it seemed up and above her.

Something crashed.

Linna turned her face. Half a field away trees were being yanked out like weeds, and strewn to the side.

She closed her eyes, so she couldn't see anymore, covered her ears, so she couldn't hear anymore. She tried to close her mind, so she couldn't think anymore.

In a few seconds it was over. Kat sat up beside her, tears streaming down her cheeks. She pointed at what remained of the nearby bush. "It touched down...over there...but not here."

Linna couldn't believe it was gone. But looking up, she saw the funnel had folded back into the sky. Only the rolling clouds remained, bumping into one another like children playing tag.

"We were lucky," she gasped, taking deep gulps of air. In the sudden quiet that followed the cyclone, her heart pumped so fast she thought it might explode.

Kat smiled weakly, her face still pale. "There could be a big rain coming too. Or maybe hail. We'd better hurry."

CHAPTER 4

Linna dropped onto the kneeler in front of the
wooden pew and offered another prayer of thanks
that the cyclone had done so little damage two weeks
ago. The rain and hail hadn't fallen on them at all. She
knew things could have been much worse, especially
since she and Kat had been caught in the open when it
touched down.

The soft murmur of people greeting one another
and making their way to the pews filled Qu'Appelle's
Immaculate Conception Roman Catholic Church. The
brick building was much newer than the church she had
attended with her family in Germany, like everything
else in this young country. The smell of new wood
mixed with that of paint made her long once again for
a town house to live in.

Reverend Maillard, a friend of Father Sauner's, was midway through his painting of the Last Supper above the altar. Linna noted the progress he'd made since last Sunday. It was going to be beautiful.

Konrad wiggled on the seat beside her, as if he was already tired of sitting. "Do you think it will start soon?" he whispered.

"Shhh," she answered, as she watched more of her community file into the church. The first evening Mass was in German and Latin, with the second in French and Latin, so everyone hurried to be on time. Mama was so relieved to be able to understand the homily, hymns, and prayers. With the English Mass in the morning, there was no danger of Linna meeting Sarah Booker or her parents, either, so she was relieved, too.

Most of the men, like Papa, wore dark suit coats even though the evening wasn't much cooler than the day had been. Their pants were heavy too, probably the same ones they wore during the winter. Some of the men were tall and others short and stout, but the faces all seemed vaguely familiar, as if she could have been back home in Colmberg.

The women, a few carrying babies, and others hustling their children into pews, wore more interesting clothes. Mama always put on her navy skirt and white blouse, but some of the other ladies had dresses that brought sunshine into the dim sanctuary. Linna wished she had something as bright as Kat's best green dress.

Instead, she smoothed her own navy skirt and listened while Papa whispered to Mama.

"See, that's Gregor, he works with me at the mill. I've told you about him – how strong he is, like a bull," Papa said.

Mama nodded. "And where does his family live?"

"He has no wife yet, but is working to bring his brothers from the old country. His parents say they'll live out their days where they are, but they want their sons to have opportunities."

Before Papa could say anything more, Father Sauner appeared at the front of the church, his long white robes rustling over the hardwood floor. Silence fell immediately.

Linna watched as the rays of the sun sneaking in the South windows settled on the shoulders of the tallest family members in front of her. She wondered if her own Papa was bathed in its glow too, further down the bench to her left. As the Mass began, she waited patiently for her favourite part – the hymns.

When the organist began she lifted her voice and let her thankfulness fill the church. Across the aisle and up a few rows, Kat turned her head and met Linna's eyes. Concentrating on hitting a high note, Linna focused on her voice, happy she'd shared her love of singing with her new friend. If only she could forgive Papa, she might be able to be truly happy in this new country.

After Mass everyone quickly dispersed as the next group began to assemble. Linna would have liked to linger by the flower bed in front and visit with Kat, but Papa had other ideas.

"Hurry along," he said, "I want to show you something before we go home."

Mama nodded, but didn't ask questions.

Konrad, his hand secured in Mama's, said, "What, Papa? Is it another horse race? I liked it there."

Papa shook his head. "No, not a horse race. Something better. Something I think Linna will like."

Linna did her best to give Papa a happy smile to try and make things better with him, while she thought about what it could be. She didn't dare to hope it was a real house, so she considered other things. Perhaps a dress from the ready-made store? But then she remembered none of the businesses were open, as she passed the first big Closed sign in the window of the General Store.

They continued up the street until they reached the Parish Hall, where a line-up of people stood outside, swatting mosquitoes and flies from their best Sunday clothes. Linna couldn't make out the words on the paper sign taped above the door, but she recognized the picture. It was a lantern slide show!

"What is it?" demanded Konrad.

"A slide show with piano music," said Papa, "of the Bible story of Ruth. Would you like to go?"

"I would," whispered Linna, feeling excitement surge through her, although she'd never been to one.

Konrad shrugged. "Me too."

Linna could hardly contain her eagerness as she danced from one foot to the other on the sidewalk. She jumped when she heard a voice behind her say, "Hello."

Turning around, she smiled. She felt almost too shy to answer the boy without Kat there as well. "Hello. You're Henry, aren't you?"

The boy nodded, his sparkling blue eyes staring into hers. They were almost exactly the same height. While she hadn't noticed the day she met him at the horse races, she saw now that one of his feet was different. It had a special wide right shoe that didn't match his left one.

"The show is very good," Henry said. "I saw it yesterday too. My father runs the projector so I come all the time."

"You're so lucky." Linna sighed.

"Henry! I need you in here," shouted a woman.

"I have to go," said Henry. "See you again."

Linna watched as he moved awkwardly through the crowd. For a second she wished she could get to know him better and be his friend, but then she remembered Sarah was his friend already.

Mama said nothing standing in the line, but held tightly to Papa's hand as he found some coins to drop into the collection box at the door when their turn came. Linna was surprised how quiet Mama had become since they arrived, and how she seemed unsure of what to do in the new land. On the ship and the train she'd led them onward, managing to get them here even with her little English, but now she waited for Papa or Linna to do everything outside the soddie.

Settling into a chair beside Konrad at the back of the packed hall, Linna held her breath in anticipation. Piano music echoed through the room, although Linna couldn't see who was playing. The music was gentle, like the sound of early morning rain on tree leaves. Over the hats of all the ladies in front of her she watched as Ruth, sickle in hand, stood alone in a field of wheat in a strange new land. Linna knew how Ruth felt. Naomi and Ruth, their black and white bodies flattened, flickered across the screen without sound. Instead, the piano provided their voices.

Linna wished she could stand and sing Ruth's story.

By the time the show ended the Parish Hall was stuffy and hot. Small clouds of cigar smoke drifted overhead, and the smell took Linna's breath away. She coughed.

Rushing out into the fresh air ahead of Mama and Papa, she ran smack into another girl. Looking up, she saw Sarah Booker's white, lace-covered dress. She turned quickly, trying to get away, but one of her buttons snagged the fragile fabric. She heard the awful sound of material tearing and stared with horror at the rip on Sarah's dress.

"You should be more careful," Sarah burst out, backing away from her.

"I...I'm..." muttered Linna. She felt like she couldn't breathe, never mind think. Her mind scrambled to find the English word she knew so well. "I'm s...s...sorry." She could tell by the anger on Sarah's face that the word wasn't enough. "I didn't...mean...to...bump..." She backed further away.

"Sarah, we're ready to go," said her prim and proper mother, stepping between them.

Sarah's eyes instantly filled with tears as one hand covered the tear on her dress and the other pointed at Linna.

"Where are your parents?" Mrs. Booker glared at Linna. "Children aren't allowed to come alone," she added with a stern voice, running her fingers over the torn sleeve of Sarah's dress, tsk-tsking with her tongue.

Papa guided Mama up behind Linna and smiled pleasantly at Mrs. Booker. Neither he nor Mama must have seen what happened; he didn't realize Linna had torn Sarah's dress. Embarrassment flooded Linna – her cheeks grew hot. She wished for a river to throw herself into, so she could disappear from sight.

"*Guten tag,*" murmured Mama, her hand gripping Papa's arm.

Mrs. Booker swerved on her fancy black shoes, ignoring Mama. Linna felt like screaming at her for being so rude to the German hello, but Papa stepped ahead and stopped to speak to her, while Mama dropped her hand.

Linna couldn't make out their words, but she heard Mrs. Booker's responding laugh. Anger flared in her as quickly as her previous embarrassment. What had Papa said?

Mama clamped one hand firmly around Linna's, dragged Konrad with the other, and started making her way through the people chatting on the street. Her lips were drawn together and her eyebrows twitched like she was angry.

Papa caught up to them in a few minutes, his footsteps clattering behind them on the new cement sidewalk. "Why are you rushing?" he asked. "I wanted you to meet Mrs. Booker. You know, I do the accounts for them each Monday."

Wrapping her fingers tightly around Mama's, Linna clenched her teeth, no longer as sorry for tearing Sarah's dress as she had been. Papa might belong in this town, but none of the rest of them did.

"She seemed unfriendly." Mama's voice quivered like she might cry.

Papa's long strides took him a few steps past Linna. "Many of the people in town would like the soddies removed. She's really very nice..." he added, almost as if he was apologizing for her meanness.

Linna turned the corner onto the dirt street that led to the German settlement. There were no cement sidewalks there, just a few blocks of wooden ones, before they too ended. It didn't seem fair at all. How could people who had more than they did, be so cruel?

The rest of the walk seemed to take forever. Linna refused to respond to anything Papa said, instead, she turned her head to watch the setting sun. The sky filled with streaks of orange and red as the yellow ball of light dropped below the horizon. Two black hawks swooped over her head, their wings flapping silently. The singsong voices of crickets began. Although she felt like racing past Papa and going to Kat's house to talk, she didn't dare. Papa was the head of the family and her duty was to obey him.

He opened the door of their soddie, where it was still cooler inside than outside. Linna followed Konrad, standing beside the open door until Mama could light the coal oil lamp in the middle of the table. With only two tiny windows, there wasn't much light after the sun had set. Once the small wick was burning, it made a soft glow. Mama also lit the big hanging lamp in the centre, so the room brightened.

Konrad seemed to not understand that everyone else was upset. "Can we play marbles, Papa?" he said. "Can we please?"

"Aren't you tired, Konrad?" said Papa, a hint of a smile on his lips. "I wish I had your energy."

Konrad used the wheedling voice he was good at, asking again, "Please play marbles with me, Papa."

Papa turned to Linna, saying nothing for a moment, then finally, "Would you like to play marbles, Linna?"

Linna shook her head slowly. It would have been fun to play for a little while before she crawled into bed, but that would make Papa think she'd forgiven him for laughing with Mrs. Booker and upsetting Mama. She knew she should thank him for taking them to the slide show, but she just couldn't.

Mama stood and reached across her bed to the shelf that held the hairbrush. "Let me brush your hair, Linna, while Papa and Konrad play marbles."

Thankfully Linna dropped down onto the soft bed beside Mama. Papa pulled the bag of marbles out and handed them to Konrad.

"I get all the blue ones," Konrad said, his voice giggly and full of excitement. "I always beat you, Papa, when I have blue." He dumped the bagful onto the small rag rug Kat had made for Linna, which lay in the middle of the dirt floor.

Papa flopped down beside Konrad, and chose red marbles that he laid out in a circle. Konrad spread his out on the opposite end.

"Me first, me first," squealed Konrad, acting more excited as the minutes passed. He picked up a cat's eye and balanced it on his upturned fist between his thumb and forefinger. With an awkward flick the marble flew through the air and landed on top of one of the red rainbows, then bounced into another one.

"I got you – I got you!" Konrad grabbed the marbles he'd hit. "I'm winning."

Papa turned his fist up and flicked his rainbow into the pile of blue ones, hitting just one of Konrad's.

Linna leaned back against Mama, feeling the stiff bristles of the brush tugging through her hair. She relaxed, watching Konrad having fun with Papa. She wished she could go back to being the little girl who had played marbles with Papa and not worried about anything else but being his little *mouse*. The way she felt was still confusing. This new Papa was so different, and she wanted to be able to talk to him again. But nothing seemed to go right. Tonight should have been perfect. She wished Sarah Booker hadn't decided to hate her and she wished she hadn't torn her lace. She wished she'd hugged Papa and thanked him for taking her before everything else happened.

Once Mama was done her hair, Linna headed towards her bed, ready to close her eyes and forget everything.

But Papa said, "Would you sing for me, Linna? I hear you outside in the evening singing. The songs are beautiful."

Linna's heart beat faster. Papa thought she sang beautifully! "Yes," she said, taking a few deep breaths and picking a *lied* to sing. She chose one about flowers by Brahms and let the words come from her heart, *"Wie sich Rebenranken schwingen."*

Papa stopped playing marbles. So did Konrad. Mama's face glowed. With each word Linna's body relaxed and all her troubles seemed to float away with the song about flowers. The more everyone smiled, the higher the notes she sang, until she felt like a songbird. It was her happiest moment since she came to Canada.

The next day she walked back into town to buy a small bag of sugar for Mama. She stopped, as she always did, at the post office. Inside the brick building she approached the elderly postmaster, who stood behind the wooden counter. "Is there any mail for Karl Mueller's family?" she asked.

A grin spread beneath the man's tiny wire-rimmed glasses as he withdrew a letter from a narrow slot in the shelving behind him. "This what you're looking for, miss? It's got a German stamp."

"Oh yes!" Linna exclaimed, reaching for the letter. The writing on the front was in Tante Karoline's big, rounded printing and the stamp was indeed, from Germany. "Thank you."

Linna hurried down the steps back onto the street, the envelope in one hand and the sugar in the other. While she really would have liked to open the letter immediately, she didn't want to be selfish. Mama and Konrad would be just as anxious as she was to hear the news from home.

She raced down the dusty road, ignoring the heat that spread through her body with the exertion.

"Mama, Mama," she called, throwing open the soddie door. "A letter! We have a letter from Tante Karoline."

Mama dropped her sewing into her lap. "Read it to me, please."

Setting the sugar on the table, Linna opened the letter, careful to keep the stamp intact for her collection. She spread out the single sheet of paper and began to read it to Mama and Konrad.

Dear Karl, Frieda, Linna and Konrad,

We miss you all very much, but we hope things are good in Canada.

There is some good news. I am getting married this fall to Adolph Schreiner. He is a farmer from Ansbach. I'll be finished working at the castle after harvest, then will be in our home. We'll be living with his parents and looking after them.

Your cousins are all growing. Little Wilhelm has taken his first steps. I can't wait to have a child of my own. Elli adds her note on the bottom of mine.

There is also some bad news. Nana's health is failing. She is very ill and spends her days in bed. Her eyes are weak and she isn't even able to knit or do her needlework, so we take turns sitting and talking to her to help her pass the time.

I hope this finds you all in good health.

All my love,
Karoline

Elli's note was short too:

I'm busy helping with the children and garden. There is lots more work to do, with Nana ill. I hope your new school is good, Linna. I miss you all, and hope you have a good life in Canada.

The world of Linna's dreams crashed to the ground. She knew Nana would not be long in this world once she was so weak. And she knew that Tante Karoline was starting a new life of her own with a husband and his family. Even Elli's letter was short, like she was already forgotten. Life in Germany went on without them. Her life was here in Canada with Papa.

CHAPTER 5

July ended with a tremendous rain that fell, day and night, for two full days. Linna felt like she might suffocate from the damp, close air inside the soddie, if a stream of water from one of the holes in the tarp-covered ceiling didn't drown her first.

By the second day of August, when she crawled out of bed, Linna was overjoyed to see the sun shining in a clear blue sky. "Hurray," she shouted, letting the door slam shut behind her as she returned from her morning trip to the outhouse. "The rain has stopped. Can I go to Kat's, Mama, can I?"

Mama paused with the pail of rainwater she was pouring into the metal washtub on the stove. "Yes, you're free to do as you please today. Konrad can go outside to play with Dieter, so you won't have to amuse him."

"And there isn't even any water to haul, since we caught enough rain in the barrels to wash clothes for days and days and days," said Linna, her voice bubbling over with happiness.

Mama smiled. "Indeed, I can wash all of the bedding and everything. The rain was truly a blessing."

While Linna didn't think they'd needed to listen to it pour out of the sky, and watch it run down the tiny windows, for two whole days, she was willing to concede, now that it was over, that the rain had been a good thing.

Gulping down a breakfast of porridge, Linna planned her day. "Maybe Kat and I can go picking Saskatoon berries again..."

"The rain may have washed them off the trees," Mama said, ripping the quilt from Linna's bed. "There weren't many left when Anke and I were picking. The raspberries are nearly ready though. Eat your breakfast Konrad, then outside to play."

It wasn't just the bedcovers that needed washing after the rain in Linna's opinion. The water had seeped in all over, drooling muddy blobs everywhere. There wasn't a single thing that seemed clean to her.

"Done," Konrad said, shoving in a spoonful so huge that bits of it ran out the corners of his mouth.

Giving his face a quick wipe, Mama opened the door to let him outside to play in his bare feet. "No sense getting his good leather shoes all covered with mud," she said, smiling as Konrad splashed through the nearest puddle.

While her feet had toughened enough to make it from the soddie to the outhouse over the hard-packed path, Linna glanced at her shoes wishfully. She knew it was likely Mama would insist hers stay inside too. "Do I have to go barefoot, Mama? The thistles hurt my feet."

"I'm sorry Linna, but if we're ever going to have enough money to have a town house someday, then we have to be careful to take care of things. The shoes stay inside until the ground is dry." With that Mama stuck out one of her own long skinny feet, and wriggled her bare toes. "Me too."

Linna laughed. "All right. Kat always has bare feet, so I can guess I can do it today too."

Bursting out of the house, Linna glanced around. She still couldn't think of it as her village, but she'd given up the idea of going back to Germany. Maybe she'd just be an immigrant forever – a transplanted person who never felt at home. Papa and Konrad seemed to be the ones who loved it here.

"Hello Anke," she called, as their neighbour emerged from her home, checking to see what Konrad and Dieter were up to.

"And what a good morning it is," Anke answered. "The sun is shining and all that rain fell to make the gardens grow. We are blessed."

Linna nodded, but wondered if a day would come when she might only worry about rain and gardens. What about her singing? What about opera? What about her dreams to do things in her life? Would they all just disappear and she'd end up like Mama and Anke, washing the mud out of everything in a sod house?

Waving goodbye to Anke, Linna hurried along the path to Kat's, enjoying the strange feel of mud squishing between her toes. For the first time since she'd arrived in Saskatchewan, the water lay in puddles everywhere, shimmering in the sunshine.

Kat was outside, hanging diapers on the clothesline. "Hello!" she shouted.

"Hello," Linna answered, trying to ignore the sounds of baby Erich sobbing inside. It seemed like one of the little ones was always crying at Kat's.

"I have a surprise," exclaimed Kat, shoving the wicker clothes basket back towards the big square washtub where her mother stood outside, rubbing a shirt up and down over the ridges on the washboard.

"If you take the baby for a walk, you can go for awhile," said Mrs. Schaeffer, her round face flushed from exertion.

Kat glanced at Linna, and she nodded. Taking Erich wasn't too bad of a chore, although his nose seemed to run an awful lot.

Inside Kat picked the sobbing infant up from the cradle, and cuddled him. "He's getting teeth," she said. "Feel here."

Linna obediently ran her fingers inside the baby's mouth, feeling two tiny ridges. "They're sharp," she said, yanking her hand back.

"Let's go," Kat said, slinging Erich onto her hip, just like her mother did. "He'll probably fall asleep if I take him to the swing and rock him."

Following obediently, Linna watched as everyone throughout the community took advantage of the abundance of water to wash things from bedsheets and quilts to long woollen dresses from their winter trunks. The light breeze caught the sheets and turned them into sails that could take a ship across the prairie. Small boys sailed pieces of wood over the puddles, crossing from one muddy continent to the other, just as they'd done with their parents.

Kat flopped down on one of the swings hung near the pegs where the men played horseshoes every night. Linna sat on the other, dragging her feet through the muddy hollow beneath it.

"So what's the surprise?" Linna asked, suddenly curious.

"You and me can go to the theatre this afternoon, that is, if your mama will let you." The words gushed out of Kat like the rain had poured out of the sky.

"Theatre? How?"

"Tonight is the Grand Concert the ladies put on every year. I had to go to the store yesterday in the rain, and I saw Henry with his mother. He invited us to go the dress rehearsal this afternoon!"

Excitement grew in Linna. Surely a concert meant music? "Have you ever been? What is it like?"

"Henry said there are singers. His uncle is in a barbershop quartet and they sing all over. His mother is making costumes and helping set everything up. And this year there's a play about two princes fighting over a kingdom. I can hardly wait."

"What about ladies...do they sing in the concert too?" whispered Linna, suddenly hopeful.

Kat thought for a second, pushing herself back and forth on the squeaky chains that held the wooden swing. Little Erich lay quiet in her arms, his head resting against her chest.

Linna stuck her toes into the mud, dragging herself to a stop. "Do they? Are there ladies singing?" she asked urgently.

"Oh yes," Kat said, her eyes brightening. "Henry said his mother made the costumes for the beautiful princesses, so they probably sing too."

Happiness surged through Linna. Music and singing, and she could go with Kat, if Mama would let her. And someday... "The dress rehearsal is this afternoon, right?"

Kat nodded. "That's why I was up so early helping Mama do all the washing, so all the work would be done when it's time. My dress is already on the clothesline drying."

Linna shot up from the swing seat. "There was a hole in the tarp over the soddie roof, so mud and yuck dripped all over my Sunday dress. I'd better run home and see if Mama has washed it yet!"

"I'm going to rock Erich a little more until he's sound asleep, so I'll see you later," Kat said, smiling brightly. "I'll come to your place about one o'clock. All right?"

Linna raced past the soddies, past the women calling out to one another in German and hanging their clothes to dry, past the children splashing in the puddles, until she reached her own home. "Mama, Mama..." she shouted breathlessly.

"What is it?" exclaimed Mama, dropping the washboard with a splash into the dirty water. "Is something wrong?"

Shaking her head, Linna searched for a way to tell Mama that would make her see how important it was for her to go. "Kat has invited me to go the dress rehearsal for tonight's concert. I need to have my Sunday dress clean and dry."

Mama stared at her for a moment. "I think we should wait and ask Papa if it's all right for you to go."

"No," said Linna, without thinking. She quickly caught her breath and tried to explain, embarrassed at her rudeness. "I mean there isn't time. He won't be home until it's over. I have to go. You can tell me it's all right. Why would we have to ask Papa? You decided for us all the four years he was gone."

"But," said Mama, shaking her head, "in Canada Papa is head of our home and he makes the decisions."

"This doesn't need a decision. It's the same as going picking Saskatoon berries with Kat. It's just something to do that doesn't cost any money." The words fell out of Linna's heart, because her head didn't have time to think what she wanted to say.

Tears stung Linna's eyes. How could Mama think of saying she had to ask Papa first? Mama knew how important singing was to her. Why couldn't she just let her go? When would she get another chance like this one living in Qu'Appelle?

Linna tried another argument. "Kat has already washed her dress and it's drying. She's younger than me and her mother is letting her go, even though there is always so much work to do with all her little brothers. Please Mama, please, I need to go..."

Mama's face softened. She said, her voice little more than a whisper, "Yes, I guess you do need to go. Papa knows how difficult it is for you in this country. I'm sure he will understand. He loves you very much, you know."

Linna glanced away. She didn't want to talk about Papa right now; her mind was on the rehearsal and the singing.

"If it is this important, I will say yes, you can go," Mama said finally.

Linna threw her arms around her mama, letting tears of happiness fall. "*Danke,* Mama, thank you so much. I will do anything you want to help you."

"I guess the first thing will be to wash your best dress."

"Then I'll help you with all the other washing!" Linna dropped her arms and rushed inside to get the dress. "I'm going to the theatre...I'm going to the theatre..."

When Kat arrived after lunch, Linna was already at the door, waiting. Her dress was still damp around the collar and waistband, but she wore it anyway. Mama had even started a fire in the stove again, so she could heat the irons to take out the wrinkles. Steam had risen into the air when the hot metal touched the cloth, but it had helped to dry the dress, and the skirt was absolutely smooth, just like Sarah's skirts always looked.

"Goodbye, Mama. Bye Konrad." Linna waved as she hurried down the path behind Kat.

"I'm so happy," Kat said. "We're going to have a wonderful afternoon."

Linna nodded, but she didn't tell Kat how difficult it had been to convince Mama. Instead she bounced along beside Kat, careful not to get any mud on her shoes or splash her dress. Kat even wore her shoes for a change.

The sun seemed hotter than it had before the rain, so by the time Linna and Kat arrived, Linna felt like a wilted flower in her best dress. There was a steady stream of people in and out of the Town Hall, so she grabbed the door and bravely followed a group of ladies inside.

"That's where they have Court," Kat whispered, pointing at the large double doors that were firmly closed.

"Really?"

Kat nodded. "There's a jail cell in the basement too, in case someone is arrested."

"We don't have to go near it, do we?" asked Linna, feeling shivers; she wasn't sure whether they were from the cool inside air or the information.

A gale of laughter erupted somewhere above them, and Kat pointed to the stairs. "Everything is upstairs. Just wait until you see!"

Grabbing the banister railing, Linna made her way up the dark wooden stairs. She was nervous until she saw Henry poke his head around the door at the top.

"Hello," he said, waving. "Come with me – I've been waiting for you. I have places for us to sit. They're almost ready to begin."

Linna followed Henry's slow gait across the floor, hardly able to take her eyes off the elegant red curtains that covered almost the entire front of the room. "Who's that?" she asked, pointing to the picture of a man at the centre.

"King Edward, he just died in May," said Henry, sliding between two rows of wooden chairs at the far side of the room. "My mother said we should stay out of the way, so we don't interrupt anything that's going on."

The stage at the front of the immense room was hidden so Linna couldn't see what was happening. Music burst sporadically out of a piano somewhere behind the curtains, as if it was taking great gasps of air and coming slowly to life.

Linna hardly knew which way to look. Surely this was even more exciting than an opera! Two ladies, wearing elegant dresses that left their shoulders bare, walked majestically toward the front of the room.

"My mother worked on those costumes," Henry said. "The lady with red hair is supposed to be Princess Imogene, and the one with dark hair plays Princess Nadine who loves Prince Hubert."

Leaning back on her chair, Linna tried to soak up everything that was going on, so she could replay it again and again in her memory once it was over. She couldn't even listen as Henry and Kat talked, instead, she concentrated on the room. As the window shades were pulled and the stage curtains opened, she felt herself become part of the show.

The back of the stage held a set painted to show the mountains of the Kingdom that Prince Leopold of Montmorence and Prince Hubert de Calavra both wanted to claim. The giant peaks went right to the top of the stage, while the front was all draped in fresh cut grass to show the richness of the land, just like the prairies with its fields of wheat.

When the first song began Linna was drawn into the music and the story it told. She watched the valiant battle of good against evil happen right before her eyes. She forgot it was a stage. She forgot it wasn't real.

"Linna," Henry said, poking her from where he stood behind her, "do you want a glass of lemonade?"

"What?" she asked, as the curtains met in the middle on the stage.

"Come back Linna, come back. It's the intermission," teased Henry. "I'll bring you some lemonade if you like."

"I'll help you," Kat said, leaping to her feet.

Linna blinked, feeling like she truly had been somewhere else for the past hour. "I could too..."

"No, you keep our seats; there are more children coming in." Henry pointed toward the entrance.

Linna's spirits plummeted. Sarah and two other girls, both dressed in fine muslin dresses, had just entered the room. Linna watched in dismay as Henry and Kat walked away, leaving her alone.

In an effort to keep her distance from the newcomers, Linna busied herself staring at the painting on the top front drape. The crowned man had been the King of England. It was strange how Canada had had a King that lived as far away as Germany, instead of one right here. This country was immense, so how could a distant King have known anything about his people or the land? He might not have known any more than she did before she arrived, so how could he have been the ruler?

Much to her dismay, she saw Sarah making her way across the room to where she sat, while her friends stood waiting in the aisle.

"Where's Henry?" Sarah asked, without even bothering to say hello.

Linna noticed that she was wearing the white lace dress again, with the sleeve mended so neatly the tear had vanished completely, and felt better. She took a second to consider Kat's advice not to let Sarah boss her around before she answered, but decided to just respond and hope Sarah would go away. "Getting lemonade," she said, her voice squeaking out more like a mouse's than a girl's.

Sarah turned without another word, and walked back to her friends. She whispered something to them, and they all pointedly turned to find places on the opposite side of the room.

Linna tried to ignore them, but she felt a hot flush of embarrassment anyway. If only she lived in town and wasn't a squatter, maybe she'd be able to face them.

Henry and Kat appeared shortly with tall glasses of cold lemonade. Linna was able to ignore Sarah and her friends since they were so far away, although some of the magic of the afternoon had disappeared. In a few minutes the play began again, with Queen Euphemia singing about having her home stolen from her by the thrall of evil.

With each word Linna felt her heart lifting higher. If only someday she could sing such a beautiful song to a

Akacsia Dowie 9-2

room full of people, she would feel her life overflowed with happiness. If only she could get up on that stage...

"She is a wonderful singer, isn't she?" whispered Henry, leaning across Kat toward Linna.

"Oh yes," she answered, her admiration flowing over into her voice. "If only I could be like her. She's the very best singer."

Kat turned her face, and whispered, "Really? Don't you recognize her in that costume? It's Sarah's mother."

CHAPTER 6

Linna dried the last plate and set it in place.

"*Danke,*" Mama said, picking up her sewing before she sat beside Papa on the empty chair.

Part of Linna thought enviously of Sarah Booker: her fine clothes, her fancy house, and above all else, her mother's beautiful singing. Another part of her knew she'd always want her own mother, even if they lived in the soddie forever. But, in between those two parts, was the one that hoped someday she could sing on the stage just like Mrs. Booker.

Behind her, Papa and Mama spoke softly, as Papa finished his stein of lager.

"I'm going to throw horseshoes for awhile. Who wants to come and watch?" Papa asked, glancing at her.

"Me, me," Konrad said, climbing onto Papa's lap.

Linna thought quickly, trying to decide how to word her answer. Papa hadn't exactly been angry that Mama let her go the concert rehearsal in town, but he hadn't been pleased, either. Now, Henry had told her about the town library that was only open on Thursday nights for an hour, and she desperately wanted to go. What was the best way to ask Papa? After singing for him last night she felt much braver.

"Linna, do you want to watch the men pitch horse-shoes?" Mama asked.

"Well," Linna said, "it would be nice to watch you, Papa. You make so many ringers," she added, showing Papa her pride in his skill at the game. "But I've been thinking about the new school here in Canada and how much I have to learn to catch up."

"What do you mean?" Papa asked.

"Well, I can speak English pretty well, but I need to be able to read it too, or I'll get behind."

Mama nodded.

Linna considered her words carefully. "The town has a library and I could borrow some books from it to help me, but it's only open tonight."

"Borrowing books costs money," Papa said shortly.

"Yes," said Linna. "But I have money from selling the Saskatoon berries with Kat, that I could use. I want to learn to read in English, so I can do well in school here."

Mama stood and hugged her. "Surely she can go, can she not?"

"Of course." Papa smiled. "I'd forgotten you would need to learn to read in English for these schools, or I could have helped you already. If you have problems you can ask me at night, for I know it pretty well already." He stooped and reached under the bed to retrieve a thick, hard-covered book, then handed it to her. "It's called *In The Days of the Comet,* by H.G. Wells. It would be too hard for you yet."

Linna was surprised. She knew Papa liked numbers, but she hadn't realized he liked to read, too. "When did you learn to read English?"

"At night, when I was alone here in Canada, wishing my family was with me," said Papa, standing. "Bankers need to read as well as do numbers. Come, let's be off."

"So, may I go?" said Linna. She stared at the book, determined to get to the library because Henry said he was going to be there, but not wanting to tell Papa her second reason.

"Yes, of course. Maybe I'll read the ones you borrow, too," Papa said, his eyes not quite so tired. "Then we can talk about them..."

Linna felt guilty, since she still couldn't bring herself to do things just with Papa, but maybe books would help like music did. Although she listened to him talking while she pretended to be asleep, she still couldn't quite forgive him for not telling them the whole truth before they arrived. Or at least that was what she told herself.

When she reached the Town Hall, Linna ran her fingers over the fine wood of the big doors into the Court Room. The library, Henry had told her, was inside that room, but she was afraid to enter. Glancing at the staircase, she half expected one of the cast of players or singers from the rehearsal to come barrelling down and burst into song. Maybe that was just what Mama would call wishful thinking.

While she stood, trying to work up the courage to go in, Henry walked through the Town Hall entrance door. "Hello Linna," he said, a big grin covering his pale face.

"Hello," said Linna, suddenly feeling shy. She'd never spent time with Henry without having Kat around. This afternoon she'd tried to convince Kat to come to the library with her, but she hadn't been successful.

Henry walked towards her with his uneven gait, which reminded Linna of a dancer ready to swing out into a fancy step. "Does it bother you?" she asked, then clapped her hand across her mouth, realizing she'd spoken the question out loud.

"My foot?" said Henry. "No, it doesn't hurt. But it means I can't do lots of things because I can't run like other children. I really wanted to learn to use snowshoes last winter with my little brother, and I couldn't. That hurts me inside."

Linna nodded. "I know how you feel."

Henry held out a book for her to look at. "This is a new one. It costs five cents per week, but you might want to read it later." He turned the handle and the Court House door squeaked open. "Let's go in."

The large desk at the front of the room drew Linna's attention. "What's the hammer for?" she asked, pointing to an object on it.

Henry walked up and tapped it against the desktop. Bang. Bang.

"Order in the court," Henry said. "It's called a gavel, and it's something judges use to get people's attention."

"You've never needed one though have you Henry?" said the librarian, glancing up from a corner where he was shelving books.

Henry nodded, then hammered the gavel one more time. "Adeline Mueller, I sentence you to...oh what shall it be? A visit to the prison below?"

Adeline felt herself grow warm with his teasing, and glanced at the librarian to see if he was upset.

The librarian ignored Henry's antics, and asked, "Did you like *The Secret Garden?*"

"Very much Mr. Struthers. I hope we can get it for the school library too, so I can read it again."

"We'll see," said Mr. Struthers, smiling. "This year's books have already arrived and I'm sure you'll find some favourites among them. Who is your new friend?"

"This is Linna, Mr. Struthers. Linna, Mr. Struthers is one of the teachers at our school."

"It's nice to meet you, sir," said Linna, trying hard to use her best English.

"You too, young lady. Now what kind of books can I help you find today?"

Linna peered into his face, hoping to find a friend. "I need to learn to read English. It must be very different from German. Henry says he'll help me before school begins."

"Ah," said Mr. Struthers, "Henry is a good choice in a helper. I'm sure you won't have any problems. Now, let's find you some good books to start with."

In a few minutes Linna had the five books she was allowed in her arms. They were all primers meant to help people learn to read. It took Henry much longer to look through the collection to choose five for himself, so Linna sat on one of the wooden chairs, flipping through the pages, while he picked up book after book, then returned it to the shelf.

Mr. Struthers said, "Let's check these out for you, Linna. I need to fill in your name and information on one of my borrower's cards, then collect your money."

As she carefully spelt out her name and information, Linna watched the librarian's face. When he asked for the location of her home, his expression never changed as he wrote German Settlement on the card. She let out her breath, feeling relieved that he, like Henry, didn't seem to mind that her family were squatters.

"Now, Adeline, that will be ten cents for two weeks. If you don't bring them back on time, I'll have to charge you late fees," Mr. Struthers said.

"Oh, I'll be here again in two weeks," Linna assured him. "By then I hope I'll be able to get harder books to read." She handed him one of her hard-earned ten-cent pieces.

Henry, his arms full with the weight of his heavier volumes, came up behind her. "I'm ready too, Mr. Struthers. I have another new one – *The Road to Oz* by L. Frank Baum. I can hardly wait to begin it!"

Before they finished, two grey-haired ladies began to examine the books, whispering to one another as they withdrew different titles from the shelves. While it wasn't a large library, it seemed everyone could find something interesting to read. Linna suddenly thought of Papa's book that he'd stored under the bed, and wished she'd looked more closely at it. Perhaps she could have chosen a new one for him. Maybe next time she would.

She skipped down the big steps out of the Town Hall, then immediately felt sorry as she turned and watched Henry painstakingly making his way step by step.

"Do you want to stop at my house for a few min-utes? I'll help you get started on the books," said Henry, not seeming to notice how rude Linna had been.

"Would you?"

"Of course. It's only 7:30, so there's quite a bit of time before dark," he said.

Matching her pace to Henry's, Linna walked down the fine cement sidewalks to where Henry lived a few blocks away. His house, while not as grand as Sarah's, was still very nice.

Wide, green-painted wooden stairs led up to the front veranda, where Henry dropped down onto a wide white porch swing. His mother, Mrs. Spencer, immediately came through the screen door, and said, "Hello, Linna. Did you get some good books at the library, Henry?"

"Yes, Mother," he answered. "I'm going to read out here with Linna for awhile. Can we have some cookies?"

Linna was a little surprised Henry's mother knew her name, since the only time she'd seen her was at the horse races, but of course Henry had probably told her they were meeting at the library. She glanced around the veranda, then hesitantly sat on the swing opposite him, setting her pile of books down between them.

The houses around her all seemed much like Henry's: tall, two-storey homes painted white with different colours of trim around the windows and on the roof. Some had black. Some had green. None had blue, like those in her own neighbourhood across the tracks.

"I brought you lemonade," Mrs. Spencer said, returning. "I thought you might be thirsty too." She handed them each a glass and a small plate of cookies.

"Thank you," said Linna quickly.

Henry echoed her thanks, and opened one of the books between them. "These are my mother's best sugar cookies." He picked one up, pointed to the book, and said, "This word is *cat* and here's its picture to help you figure it out."

Linna let the cookie melt in her mouth, savouring the sweetness, then took a big sip of the tangy lemonade. It was a moment until she could concentrate on what Henry was showing her in the book. Before she realized it an hour had passed, and the sun was sinking low in the sky.

"Oh dear," said Mrs. Spencer, opening the door again. "You really must hurry home, Linna, or you'll be after curfew. I intended to send you a little earlier!"

Linna blinked, not really sure what the word *curfew* meant. "I'm sorry, I don't understand," she said, feeling flustered.

"The curfew means children under fourteen, not accompanied by their parents, must be home by the time the Anglican Parish Hall bell rings at 9 p.m. Or their parents are fined a dollar," answered Mrs. Spencer.

"Oh no!" exclaimed Linna, gathering her armful of books. A dollar was a lot of money, more than enough to buy material for a new dress or a bag of flour to make bread.

Henry handed Linna the book they'd been working through. "If you need more help come to visit me again."

"I will," she said, hastily standing. "Thank you, Henry, for all your help. Thank you too, Mrs. Spencer, for your cookies and lemonade. They were wonderful."

Without a backwards glance, Linna hurried down the steps to the street. Around her, the town's few street lights blinked to life, as the power from the Qu'Appelle Electric Light Company was turned on. A light magically came on in the window of a house to her right.

On the western horizon the sun dropped into the red-streaked sky, which meant the next day would surely be windy. There was little going on, although she heard the yips of two dogs somewhere behind. Her feet thudded against the sidewalk, as she hurried down Main Street, then turned to take the road home past the elevators. Small black flies swarmed around her face, while mosquitoes hovered over her bare arms, like they were waiting for her face to turn away so they could take a bite.

A car, its engine purring noisily, turned a corner in front of her. A boy a little bigger than she pedaled his bicycle furiously past, no doubt rushing home before the curfew too.

Her mind raced with the evening's events, seeing the English words and trying to relate them to the way they were written in German. Would she really be able to figure out the secrets of reading in this new language before school began? She picked up her pace, until she was almost running to beat the curfew.

As she reached the mill, the streetlight flickered, then went out. There were, Papa had said in his nightly talks with Mama, problems with the power the mill owner was providing for the town. It was costing him too much money and he wasn't able to keep it going when he should. Lights that were supposed to be on until 11:30 at night on weekdays sometimes went on and off, sometimes didn't come on at all, if his coal supply hadn't arrived on time. Of course it didn't matter to the squatters, because they lived on their side of the railway tracks. They didn't have any electricity.

But Papa, along with many of the other men in their community, worked for the mill, so they worried about their jobs. No business could keep open if it was losing money. No bank would wait to collect its money. Linna hoped the townspeople would just agree to pay more for their power. They were so lucky to have it, while she had none.

The church bells rang as she crossed the railroad tracks. It was 9 p.m. and nearly dark. A coyote howled in the distance, as if it was answering the town bells with a challenge of its own.

Just before she reached the settlement she heard voices. Her hands, where they gripped the books, quivered. What if it was the Town Constable, ready to seize her and take her home to her parents?

"Who's running?" someone shouted. "Is that you?"

Linna ignored the challenge, too scared to even turn around to look. She ran.

"Wait, slow down," came another voice, even louder than the first.

She clutched her books tighter to her chest, feeling her heart throbbing wildly beneath them. Under her feet the lumps and bumps of the dirt road disappeared, like she was floating above them. She was almost there!

The settlement loomed closer.

She ran harder.

Finally, she ducked behind the first soddie and stopped. Her whole body shook as she panted for air.

The voices, now further away, were harder to understand. "...not Sammy...just a girl...squatter..."

They were just boys, Linna realized as her heartbeat slowed, probably looking for their friend Sammy. It wasn't the Town Constable.

Relief flooded her, but with it came dread about what her father would say when she reached home. She knew it was much too late to be returning. They would have worried, and she felt guilty for that.

Picking her way over the path through the settlement in the dark, she listened to the sounds of families readying for bed. Dim candlelight shone through the windows, creating willowy shadows inside. At her own door, she paused, straightened the books in her arms, and then turned the doorknob.

Linna saw relief spread across Mama's face at the same time as Papa's reddened with anger.

"Where have you been?" he demanded.

Konrad quickly pulled the covers over his head

where he lay on the bottom bunk. Linna wished she could do the same tonight.

Instead she squared her shoulders and glared at Papa. "Getting books and trying to learn how to read English so I can fit into your new country," she said, flinging the words. "Maybe the other children won't all hate me if I can read, even though I am just a squatter from the wrong end of town."

CHAPTER 7

Friday morning, Linna waited until Papa left for the mill before she climbed out of bed and dressed for the day. After last night's argument, she wasn't ready to talk to him.

"*Guten morgen,*" said Mama. "Show me your books."

While she ate her porridge, Linna was pleased to read Mama the words she'd learned working with Henry. "This is *dog.* And this is *rabbit,* that's Henry's favourite picture."

"Who is Henry?" asked Mama, glancing up from the book. A teasing twinkle filled her eyes.

Linna felt her face grow warm. "A boy who will be in my grade at school. Kat knows him and he's been nice to us," she said quickly. Linna wasn't sure how much more to tell Mama about the children around

Qu'Appelle. It would make her very sad to know how mean Sarah and her friends had been.

Mama, however, was still curious. "He lives in town?"

"Yes, in a nice house on the Main Street, past the businesses. It took me a very long time to run home from there. His mother meant to tell me earlier that it was time to go, but she forgot."

"You met his mother?"

"Oh yes," Linna nodded. "She gave me some sugar cookies." Linna was careful not to mention the curfew, since it would worry Mama even more. Now that she knew about it, she'd just make sure she was always home long before the church bells rang at night.

"So what does he look like, this Henry?" asked Mama, more curious than ever.

"Well, he has red curly hair and freckles."

"And what does he like to do?"

"He teases sometimes, like Papa used to, and he reads...he doesn't do things like other boys, because he has one foot that isn't like the other one. Kat told me it was called a club foot."

"Then I'm glad you're his friend," said Mama. "Being different is no reason..." But before she could finish, Konrad burst through the door.

"Come! Run!" Konrad screamed.

"What is it?" asked Linna, scared by the expression on his face.

"Outside, outside," he shouted, waving his arm at something she couldn't see.

Mama leapt to her feet, and Linna followed. When she burst through the door she saw immediately what Konrad meant. There was smoke, huge billowing clouds of it, drifting over the railroad tracks.

Around the community, people shouted, *"Feuer!"*

"Is it the train?"

"Maybe..."

"Nein, the *walzwerk!"*

At the words, Mama's face turned whiter than a cup of milk. Papa had been gone for an hour – he was working inside the mill.

Awful thoughts and feelings flooded through Linna. Why hadn't she explained to Papa last night, instead of yelling at him? Why must she continuously try to punish him?

"Come," said Mama, dragging Konrad by the arm. "Linna, you too. We must see what's happening."

Anke, hugging Dieter to her, emerged from her soddie to stare at the women and children hurrying past. "What's going on?"

"Feuer!" said Mama, turning back to Anke. "The *walzwerk.* I'm going to see."

Kat appeared, almost as if out of nowhere, and grabbed Linna's arm. "My Papa's at work. Is yours?"

Linna nodded. "We're going to see what's happening. Come with us."

They joined a throng of a dozen or so women, their loose housedresses flapping as they raced along carrying and dragging crying toddlers. The closer they came to the railway line the more acrid the smell of smoke became, as the cloud drifted further over the town.

Linna tripped over small rocks, her eyes focused on the billowing smoke instead of where she was going.

A panic-filled voice rang out, "The mill is on fire!"

"The mill is on fire!" shouted the people they met, although by then it was obvious.

The bells that had rung out time for the curfew last night sounded again, alerting the townspeople to the disaster taking place.

By the time she reached the train tracks, Linna felt the terrible heat from the fire. Fear that Papa was still inside the mill drove her, urging her to race ahead of Mama.

The fire engine rolled down the street towards them. Men from the town raced behind with more pails and shovels.

"See the new fire engine," panted Kat, stopping to catch her breath. "The town got the engine after the Furniture Store burned down a couple of years ago. They made everyone on Main Street build their buildings of bricks, too."

"That didn't help the mill," Linna said. Flames shot out its upper floor, burning bright orange as they licked at the walls.

She scanned the throng of men splashing pails of water on the building. Papa didn't seem to be anywhere. Her heart caught in her throat. What if something happened to Papa? What if...

Then suddenly there he was dumping his pail onto the front of the building.

Her legs nearly collapsed under her as she saw that he was safe, at least for now.

"I have to tell Mama," she cried, turning around to retrace her steps, only to find Mama right beside her.

Tears streamed down Mama's face, as she pulled Linna to her. "The workers are all out," she said. "Anke asked, and they're all out."

Linna nodded, clutching Mama's hand in her own. "Papa's over there." She pointed at the men, whose faces were rapidly becoming difficult to tell apart as the soot from the fire settled in the air.

"There's my Papa," panted Kat, grabbing Linna's arm. "He's safe too!"

Around them women set their children on the ground, and threw their arms around one another. Tears of relief streamed down faces, as they turned once again to the suffocating heat of the fire.

The fire engine, a four-wheeled carriage, rolled past them with its double cylinder of water containers. Two men leapt to help pull out the long fire hose and turn the spray on the building.

Konrad stood still watching the contraption as the water flew into the flames. "I think," he said, quite seriously, "I'll fight fires when I grow up."

"Me too," said Dieter, pointing at the bright red engine.

"Get back, please, women and children! Move back," shouted one of the mill workers, waving his arms at the growing crowd. "It's not safe!"

Linna and Kat fell in with the others, stepping backwards away from the ever-increasing heat.

"It's the metal sheathing on the mill," said one elderly man, hobbling along with his cane. "It's holding the flames inside, along with all the shooting sparks, otherwise we'd have to worry about this whole street burning down."

Indeed, as Linna watched, a group of men rushed into a nearby house and began to remove the family's possessions. Out came the same things her family had packed into their trunk to bring to Canada: pictures, ornaments, and papers. Then out came bigger things, like tables, chairs, and beds. More men ran with pails from the nearby well, splashing water on the walls to keep the flying sparks from bursting into flames.

Linna felt anguish for those who might lose their property before the day was over, and fear for those near the inferno.

Henry appeared, then, separated from the crowd. "It's awful, isn't it?" he said, leading Linna and Kat away to talk.

"The men are safe though," said Kat. "Nobody has been hurt yet."

"I'm glad," Henry replied. "The fire that took the felt factory this spring was awful. I don't know why our town has to have so many fires."

"Me either," said Kat.

Linna said nothing, thinking of the water that flowed through Germany and the many stone buildings. If only Qu'Appelle had more water, maybe it would be easier to fight the fires when one did start. As it was the men could only run with buckets from the closest wells. The fire engine went further away still to fill its tanks, then had to race back. There wasn't enough to stop the raging fire.

The mill burned on and on for hours and hours, until it was well into the afternoon. Henry stayed for only a short while, until his mother called him to go. Finally, as Kat and Linna sat in the shade of a half-grown poplar tree a ways down the street, they heard the crash of the frame collapsing inside the metal siding. The burning roof dropped as though the arms that held it had let go, sending up curls of thick black smoke.

Linna stopped breathing for a moment. Her lungs filled, not with smoke, but fear. The seconds ticked by. Clouds of smoke billowed out of the mound that had been the mill. Finally she saw Papa still safe, throwing water at the flames.

The wind seemed to shift direction, so it blew right into Linna's face. "We have to move." She rose, pulling Kat with her.

"Let's go down there beside the church ladies," Kat said. "Maybe we'll hear more about how much longer they think it will last."

Tired after the long day's vigil, since she'd promised to watch, then run home with news for Mama if anything happened, Linna nodded.

Three women hovered around a wooden table spread out with crocks and plates of food. Linna's stomach rumbled at the sight of the rhubarb pies, but knew the food was for the men who were working so hard on the fire.

"The building was better built than most," said one of the fire fighters, who stood in front of the table. He took great gulps of iced tea from a tin cup, then wiped a clean streak from the wetness around his mouth across his sooty face. His eyes seemed tired, like it was the middle of the night instead of the afternoon.

"What caused it, do they think?" asked one of the women.

"Spark flying off the engine from the early train, maybe," he said, taking a giant bite of pie. "Some are saying it might have been spontaneous combustion from the contents inside. Maybe we'll never know."

"Those trains are a problem all right," said the woman.

Another nodded. "Yes, I've heard they cause grass fires right down the rail line in dry years."

"Whatever the cause, it's a big loss. Lots of jobs will be gone."

Linna gasped. Why hadn't she thought of Papa having no job, as she watched the mill burn? What would they do now? They couldn't survive on the money he earned working a few nights a week doing business books. When he had lost his job in Germany, they'd moved to Canada. Where could they go from here? Where was the land of opportunity for men who wanted to work in banks or doing accounts, instead of building things or farming the earth?

As if she could read her thoughts, Sarah Booker stepped in front of Kat. She said quietly, "Mostly the jobs of squatters are gone, so maybe the squatters will go too."

"Lots of townspeople worked there too," Kat said, defiantly planting her hands on her hips.

"My father will hire many of them to help with harvest," Sarah responded. "He said that at lunch today."

But Kat wasn't about to give up. "And what about your electricity? You won't have any fancy lights unless somebody else takes over the power plant will you?"

Sarah's face dropped. Clearly she hadn't thought of that.

Linna added in a soft voice, "You'll have to read by candlelight like we do, and walk down your streets in the dark." She already knew what a difference that could make after coming home last night.

"Sarah dear," called one of the ladies, "where's your mother? Did she send a message?"

Sarah whirled around without saying another word, and approached the ladies. "Yes, she's got another dozen pies cooking, and will send some as soon as they're done. She asked if that would be enough?"

"Thank your Mama for me," said the fire fighter. "Those sure were good pies, but I'd better get back to work."

Beaming, Sarah answered, "Mama makes the best pies around. She always wins on Fair Day."

One of the women answered Sarah's question. "I think that should be good, as we have more coming from a few others. The fire's settling down and they've been able to keep it from spreading. Unless a strong wind comes up, the rest of the street is safe."

"Thank you Ma'am," Sarah said, smiling sweetly at the women, then hurrying towards her bicycle. "I'll tell my mother."

For a minute Linna had a hard time believing the Sarah who spoke to the church ladies was the same one they'd been talking to. It seemed like she was two different people.

"Maybe we should go home too," suggested Kat.

Linna agreed. Together they kept well past the edge of the firefighters, watching as more gallons of water were still being dumped onto the building. The flames no longer shot skyward, but burned quietly, more like the flame of a candle with its wick nearly gone.

It was quiet in the little settlement, with only a few sounds of crying babies to interrupt the cawing of crows and the rustle of the wind through the cornstalks.

"See you later," Kat said, leaving Linna at her home.

Too tired to talk, Linna simply nodded, opened the door to the welcome coolness and waved.

"Is there news?" asked Mama.

"The frame inside the mill has collapsed and the fire is dying down. The firefighters kept it from spreading to other houses."

"Ich bedanke mich!" Mama heaved a sigh of relief. "Is that it then?"

"They need to watch in case a wind comes up that could blow the sparks around, so they're still working on it." Linna leaned into Mama's arms, trying hard not to cry.

"It's all right," Mama said. "Nobody was hurt. It was just a building, remember, just a building. They can build another."

"But Mama, what about Papa's job? What if they don't build another mill? How will he get money to buy our food? Our clothes? Surely his bookkeeping isn't enough!" asked Linna. Suddenly a new wooden house didn't seem nearly as important as other things.

"Don't worry about it, that's for grown-ups to think about, not girls," Mama said. "Papa managed when he came to this country alone, without even knowing how to speak English well. Now he's sure to have no trouble."

"But there will be lots of men looking for jobs if the mill doesn't rebuild. Where will they all find work? What about Kat's Papa? And Anke's husband? And all the men who work in the town?"

"Never mind. Have something to eat, then lie down for a little rest and you'll feel better."

As Linna wiggled under her blanket she took a deep breath of the cool air inside the soddie. It smelt so good after the smoke and heat of the fire. At least, she reassured herself, a soddie couldn't burn. She'd never have to worry about flames shooting out its windows.

When she awoke, hours later, Papa sat at the table, his face still black and weary from fighting fire. She leapt from the bed, landing on the floor with a thud.

"Awake, I see," Papa said. "Your eyes are red from all the smoke."

Mama turned quickly, peering into her face. "Yes, they do look sore. Are you all right?"

Linna smiled, her heart full of happiness. Her Papa was all right! That was all she needed to know. "Of course I'm all right. Look how red Papa's eyes are — much worse than mine, probably."

"You're right," Mama said. "And I never even noticed; I was just happy to have him back without any injuries."

"We're all glad of that," Papa said quietly. "Konrad, what are you building?"

Linna glanced at the floor where Konrad had his dominoes all laid out in a long row.

"A new town," Konrad said. "One that doesn't have fires to burn things down."

Sarah's taunts popped into Linna's mind, and she turned to Papa. "What will you do without the mill? Will we have to move again?"

Papa ran his fingers through his hair. "We'll see."

"But Papa, what about your job..."

"We'll see," he said again, firmly, like the discussion had ended whether Linna was ready or not. "Show me your library books. Perhaps Konrad would be interested too."

So Linna went to her shelf and pulled down the books with their English words and little pictures. Pulling a chair up to the table, she laid the book out in the glow of the coal oil lamp. Henry's lessons of the night before had worked well, for she was able to read many of the pages.

Mama put some cold venison and slices of buttered bread on a plate, so Linna took big bites between words, washing the food down with water.

Running her fingers over a page in the book, Linna looked at the word. "Home," she read, watching the eerie shadows from the lamp on the newspapered walls.

CHAPTER 8

The fire smouldered just over the railroad tracks for several days before the men could finally begin to clean up the mess. Papa was one of the ones allowed to stay on to do the job, while Kat's father wasn't. They'd already announced there wasn't enough insurance money to rebuild the mill. The only thing that remained was to salvage what they could. Papa went to the owner's house to finish up the accounts and see if the insurance money would cover the bills. It wouldn't.

Supper on Papa's last day of work was quiet. The whole German community was quiet.

"We should give God thanks," Mama said, preparing to say grace before their supper.

The meal was simple, even more so than usual. Mama was trying to conserve whatever money they had. The corn from the garden was ready, so four long cobs filled the plate in the middle of the table. The side pork, though, instead of being in a dish of its own, was mixed in with the potatoes to make it go further.

Linna smeared a little butter over her corn, grabbed one end of the cob in each hand and raised it to her mouth. "Um," she said, nibbling off the sweet kernels. "Corn is the best food in the world."

Papa grinned, his face covered with greasy spots. "It's almost as good as leftover porridge fried up with pork fat."

Knowing Papa was teasing her, Linna still couldn't keep from smiling back. "You can eat all of that you want, but I'll have corn instead." She wondered though, if the winter might not bring a lot of meals of porridge.

Once she was done the supper dishes she left for Kat's house. As the days continued to get shorter, the evenings cooled off earlier and earlier, so she had grabbed a sweater from the trunk for the first time today. Fall and school had always come together, even back home in Germany.

Kat was outside her house, taking in the last of the clothes from the line. "Just a minute," she said, "I'm almost done."

Rather than following her into the crowded little house, Linna leaned against the clothesline post and stared out at the prairie. A few bright yellow golden asters and blue beardtongue danced with brown blades of grass. Even the trees' leaves were fading, getting ready for the next season. Overhead she noticed a flock of Canada geese flying in the shape of a V, instead of singly as they'd done all summer. Fall was definitely coming. Everything would change again.

Kat emerged from her house, her face looking sad, and immediately began walking. Linna followed, wondering what was wrong.

When they reached the swings, Kat flopped onto one of the seats. There were no men or boys playing horseshoes. It seemed as though the spirit of the community had disappeared in the smoke of the fire. Linna stared at her friend, worried by the tears in her eyes.

"We're moving," Kat said abruptly, kicking a rock in the dip below the swing.

Linna's heart fell, just like the framework of the mill crashing in. "When?"

"Monday. We're going to Sunday night church services, then, leaving when it gets light. We're getting a horse and wagon on Saturday from a farmer."

"But," Linna protested, "so soon? Where? What will your family do?"

"Papa has decided to homestead so we will have land. We're going north to a German community at someplace called Muenster."

"I don't want you to go," whispered Linna, knowing she sounded selfish. But how could she lose Kat now, before school began? Who would she have for a best friend — she didn't even know any other girls besides

Sarah. And how could she stand up to Sarah on her own?

Tears streamed down Kat's face, and she gulped when she answered, "I don't want to move either. But Papa is tired of looking for work. He says at least on the land we can have a cow and grow our own food. The boys will have a future too."

"What about you?" demanded Linna. "Who will you have?"

"Maybe nobody," Kat whispered, "just Mama and the boys."

Linna sat on the other swing, next to Kat. She lifted her feet and pushed off, moving back and forth with the same rhythm. They didn't say much more. What else could she talk about? It was a daughter's duty to do whatever her parents wanted, just as she'd come to Canada. She hated the fires, and she hated Qu'Appelle, where they seemed to happen much too often.

"At least you'll be here for the Fair on Saturday," Linna said. "We can still go together."

Kat nodded. "Yes, we'll have fun together at the Fair."

Linna sang one of Brangäne's parts from *Tristam und Isolde* for Kat, trying to let her voice show how she felt when she came to the words, "we hailed the happy day."

Kat said nothing, but let the tears stream down her face.

• • •

IT WAS BRIGHT AND SUNNY, just like most of the days of Saskatchewan's summer had been. Linna jumped out of bed determined to make the most of the day with Kat. They would have so much fun it would be a day they would remember forever!

The fairgrounds were even busier than they'd been on July first for the big horse race. Along with people there were animals for the stock shows: horses, cows, even chickens. A new permanent poultry building had been erected in time for the fair.

"What should we do first?" asked Linna. The hustle and bustle made her even more excited.

"Let's look at the garden vegetables and see who won for the biggest tomatoes. Then we'll see if anybody beat Sarah's mother for the best pie."

Linna followed Kat through the exhibits, carefully taking note of the names marked beside the red, blue, and white ribbons. Someday, she decided, her name would be next to a red one.

"Do you think this Mary Spencer is Henry's mother?" she asked, as she stepped in front of a pair of older ladies discussing what variety of potatoes were on the display plate. It was a fine glass plate, big enough to hold several potatoes; a cob of corn; a handful of peas, some shelled; both green and yellow beans; and some round white onions.

Kat nodded. "His mother wins lots of prizes for her garden."

The next table held flower arrangements and Linna felt herself drawn, as if by an invisible piece of string, to stand beside the vases. "I've never seen so many different kinds of flowers – not even at Castle Colmberg!"

Groaning, Kat answered, "You're lucky you never had Miss Jelly for a teacher or you'd be able to spell dozens of flower names and identify them all!"

School. A little of Linna's excitement disappeared at the reminder that she'd have to face all the new children at the school, and Sarah Booker, without Kat. But she straightened her shoulders, determined that nothing mattered but having a good time today.

She pinched her nose shut while they walked through the new poultry building, wondering why everyone made such a fuss about chickens, ducks, and turkeys anyway. She could still hear the cackling when they were in the cattle area, listening to the bulls bellow. Although she didn't ask, and spoil their fun, she wondered how Kat felt about moving to a farm to raise all of these noisy, smelly animals.

As they walked around Kat stopped every few minutes to talk to other children, while Linna stood at a distance. She wanted to let Kat say goodbye on her own. She remembered with sadness her own last day before leaving Germany. She wondered, for the first time in days, what Elli was doing. A little bit of guilt seeped into her good mood, as she realized that she had almost forgotten about her life before Canada, at least for a time. Maybe that meant she was settling in. She hoped so.

Sticking her face under the spout of the pump at the well, she enjoyed the splash of cold water as she quenched her thirst.

"Hello, Linna," Henry said, his face crinkling with laughter.

Embarrassed to be caught doing such an unladylike thing, Linna quickly said, "It's so hot...."

Kat, who never worried about such things, quickly stuck her face into the water to catch the last stream herself. "Um, that was so good. Hello Henry."

"Are you really moving Kat?" asked Henry, his face suddenly serious.

Kat nodded. "Early on Monday morning. How did you hear? I've been looking for you to tell you."

"Sarah told me." Henry stared off in the opposite direction, his attention seemingly attracted by cheering at the show ring where the cattle had been parading.

Linna guessed Henry didn't want to tell Kat what else Sarah had said, but she could imagine it herself.

"I should have known Sarah would find out. She likes to know everything about everybody," murmured Kat. "Oh well, at least she's not moving to Muenster."

Anxious to change the subject, Linna asked, "Did you finish your new books yet Henry? I've read all mine through once." Pride filled her voice. Once she'd sat down with the books to study them, the language had come easily.

Henry smiled. "Nearly. We'll be able to go the library again next week."

Kat, never one to let what was on her mind go unspoken, added, "You'll have to be Linna's best friend when I move Henry. Make her stand up to Sarah when school starts."

A flush moved up Linna's face. While she'd been hoping for exactly that, she'd never have been able to say it.

"Of course," Henry responded, as if there was no real need to discuss it. "It's nearly time for the sports events. I'm so glad they're back this year, after the organizers took them out last year. I like to watch and see who wins."

Linna was sure she detected a hint of longing in Henry's voice, but didn't comment. "What kind of sports?"

"Foot races, high jump, long jump, and even throwing a cricket ball. I do that one, although my arm isn't really strong enough to ever win." He grinned. "But it's fun to try!"

Linna watched as families spread out quilts and picnic baskets in the shade of the few trees at the edge of the grounds. Those who had brought teams and wagons opened baskets on the back, and handed children cups of water and pieces of cold fried chicken. Laughter carried on the breeze like dandelion seeds.

The children were lining up for foot races when Linna, Kat and Henry reached that part of the field.

"Eleven-year-old girls," yelled a deep voice, "eleven-year-old girls."

"That's you Kat. Maybe I should try to make you angry – you run fastest when you're upset," teased Henry.

Kat just laughed and ran to the starting line, her dark hair bouncing and bright eyes filled with fun. She put her toe inside the white powdered line, placing the other leg behind her to push off when the whistle blew. Another dozen girls took their places beside her, some chucking heavy leather shoes behind them at the sight of Kat's bare feet.

"You can do it Kat," shouted Henry.

"Run hard, Kat," called Linna, crossing her fingers behind her back for luck. Surely Kat deserved to win a red ribbon on her second-last day in Qu'Appelle.

A crowd of children quickly gathered around Linna and Henry, although Linna didn't know any of them.

The starter, a thin man dressed in grey pants with a striped vest over his white shirt, put a whistle to his lips. "Ready! Set!" He blew it.

At the first sound Kat was off, racing like the wind across the level piece of prairie. She took an early lead, but the hundred-yard mark was a long distance ahead. Another girl, thin and tiny, her red dress fluttering up past her knees, edged up beside her.

"Go Kat. Run," screamed Linna, her heart in the race with her "You can do it!"

Around her other voices cheered for different girls. "Harder, Elsie, harder!"

"Go Janie, go!"

Henry shouted, "You can do it, Kat. I know you can do it."

As the finish neared Kat and the girl in red were exactly even. Linna felt her heart in her throat. "Do it Kat," she whispered.

The crowd roared around her, as more and more people gathered to watch.

The girls shot past the judges. Silence fell. From where Linna stood it had been impossible to tell who won. At the other end Kat stared at the judges. So did the girl in red. Time stood still. The judges, their white shirts showing wet stains under the arms, conferred for a minute, then walked to the competitors. One grabbed Kat's arm and held it up for all the crowd to see.

Linna cheered until tears ran down her cheeks.

The eleven-year-old boys raced next, which gave Linna a chance to hug Kat and stare admiringly at her red ribbon. Before Linna knew it, they were calling the twelve-year-old girls.

"Are you racing Linna?" asked Henry. "We'll cheer for you."

Linna stared at the distance she would have to race, and knew it was likely she'd run out of breath. But she decided, looking at her friends' faces, that she'd try anyway.

Sarah Booker also appeared out of the crowd at the starter's call. Linna was careful to line up at the opposite end. She glanced down at her worn leather shoes, undecided about whether to run with them on or take them off. Her feet were still not used to going barefoot on the stubbly prairie grass for any distance. She left her shoes on.

As she expected, Linna was far from the front of the pack of girls when the race ended.

In the jumble of people Linna ended up beside the girls getting their ribbons. Sarah took the blue she'd won for second, and handed it to her mother, her eyes looking blurry with tears. Linna was close enough to hear Mrs. Booker say, "You would have won, Sarah, if you'd been paying closer attention to the starter's whistle. Myra had three steps in before you even moved."

Linna ignored them and hurried back to her friends. She wondered why winning a red ribbon in a race, instead of blue, would seem so important to Mrs. Booker. If it had been something to do with singing, then she wouldn't have been surprised.

After the racing, the next event was the cricket ball throw and Henry hurried to stand with the twelve-year-old boys to wait for his turn.

"I hope Henry wins," Kat said.

"Me too," added Linna. If she could have one wish right now, she would wish for Henry's leg to be all right, so he could do all the things others did. But if not, maybe he could win this event for Kat's last Fair with them.

Each boy threw the ball three times, while a group of adults marked their spots in the field. One dark-haired boy wound up his arm and let it go flying backwards. Everyone laughed, even the boy. Another huffed and puffed up his cheeks until his face turned red, but when he let the ball go, it went straight up in the air and came down in almost exactly the same spot. When everyone laughed he turned and stormed away, disappearing into the crowd, rather than taking his second shot.

Henry grabbed the ball when his name was called and carefully examined the field, as if measuring everything in his mind. There was only one more boy after him, so he could see exactly how far he had to throw to get a ribbon.

 Linna watched nervously as he warmed up his arm, testing the weight of the ball in his hand, and took aim. At the final moment, though, when he let the ball fly, she closed her eyes, afraid to see what happened. A second later, at loud cheers, she opened them quickly. Henry's ball had flown the furthest and the judge was putting a mark on his spot!

Across from her, amidst the hurrahs of the crowd, Linna saw happiness glowing on Mrs. Spencer's face, and knew how pleased she must be for Henry.

His next two balls landed much shorter, so he didn't improve his spot. When she saw the next participant, Linna's heart dropped. He was at least a foot taller than Henry, with big muscular arms and a strong, husky body. Surely he could throw much further.

The big boy didn't take any time to warm up at all; he simply stepped up to the mark and let the ball fly. It landed right behind Henry's. The spectators groaned, watching it roll a little. Linna was sure the next one would have to go further. It didn't. And the third one fell shorter still.

Jumping up and down, holding one another's arms, Linna and Kat roared with the crowd as Henry reached out to accept his first prize red ribbon.

Linna had never felt happier.

CHAPTER 9

Sunrise on the prairies would have been a beautiful sight for Linna if she hadn't been saying goodbye to Kat. She watched as the orange ball rose in the red-streaked eastern sky. Kat's family would have a calm day to begin their journey.

Everything was already loaded into the wagon, except the children, when Linna arrived at her friend's house. It was a lumpy load, with coats and blankets squished around trunks and wooden crates. During the week or more it would take them to get as far north as Muenster, the family would have to camp under the wagon at night. Linna shuddered, thinking of the howling coyotes being right up close.

Kat came out of the house, lugging baby Erich in her arms. "Goodbye, Linna. I'll miss you."

"I'll miss you, too," Linna whispered back, gulping down the sobs she felt rising in her throat. "You'll be my friend forever."

Kat nodded, handing the baby to her mother who tucked him into a spot right behind the wagon seat.

Linna stared at Kat, trying to memorize every detail of her suntanned face, as she'd done with Elli's. How could she manage without a friend? She grabbed Kat's hands and held them.

"I'm sorry girls, but it's time to go," Mrs. Schaeffer said gently. She swung herself up onto the single seat at the front of the wagon, beside Kat's father, wiggling over to make room for Kat too.

Tears rolled down Linna's face as she watched Mr. Schaeffer jingle the reins, and call, "Giddup Star, let's go." The big old horse strained to get the heavy load moving.

Kat turned on the wagon seat, waving until Linna couldn't see her any longer in the distance.

"Goodbye," she whispered, trudging home.

Once there, Linna flopped back into her bed, too sad to want to do anything but cry softly and fall asleep. Papa opened his mouth to say something, then closed it again without making a sound. Mama gave her a hug, then pulled the blanket over her.

When she awoke hours later, the house was quiet. "Where are Konrad and Papa?" she asked, as she climbed out of bed.

"Konrad is playing with Dieter, and Papa has got some carpentry work to do." Mama's voice sounded happy, not nearly as tired as it had since the mill burned.

Linna took the piece of buttered bread she offered, and sat at the table. The day stretched out before her as long and empty as the ocean voyage had been when she was trapped on the ship.

"Linna," Mama said. "I need some things from the store. Could you get them this afternoon for me?"

"Of course Mama," she answered automatically. "I don't have much else to do." The fact was, she always did Mama's shopping, mostly because Mama still had a hard time with English and didn't want to try talking to the shopkeepers. Sometimes they went together and sometimes Linna went alone, but she was always the one who did the speaking. She couldn't help but feel sad for Mama, who struggled so hard to understand what was going on in Canada.

The day, as the red sky at dawn had promised, was still; something that rarely happened in Saskatchewan, as Linna had discovered over the summer. Without the wind it was quiet except for the clunking and banging from the grain elevators.

Her first stop was the Post Office, to see if there was another letter yet from Tante Karoline. The Postmaster smiled, shook his head, and disappeared, once he'd checked for a letter for the Mueller family.

Stepping out of the Post Office, she ran smack into Henry, who was going in. "Hello."

"Hello, Linna," he said, staring at her. "I have to mail this letter for my mother. Will you wait for me?"

"Of course," Linna replied, pleased to have run into him. Mother had told her not to worry about hurrying home, so she was free to do what she wanted.

The street was busy, as usual. A man in front of the store carried a bag of flour and tossed in his wagon. His horse, tied at the hitching post, turned its head back as if to tell him to hurry up.

"Finished," Henry said, closing the Post Office door behind him. "I'm going to sneak into the meeting at the Town Hall this afternoon." He grinned. "Do you want to come with me?"

Linna, more cautious than Henry seemed to be, had questions before she could agree to participate. "Are children allowed?"

"Well, the sign doesn't say they aren't," Henry said. "When I asked my mother if I could go, she just said I'd likely find it boring, but that as long as I didn't get in the way of the grownups it shouldn't be a problem."

"What's the meeting for?"

"It's the Women's Christian Temperance Union having speakers from Regina." Henry's eyes glowed with excitement. "I've been reading about them in the newspaper and I really want to see them. I think, when

I'm grown, that I may want to go into the law or politics, so the meeting is for my education."

Linna considered Henry's words for a minute. Yes, she decided, he would make a good lawyer or politician, because he listened to everyone.

Although she had no idea what a Temperance Union might be for, she agreed to go with him. "But if they say children aren't allowed, then I'll have to go home. I don't want to do anything to make Mama or Papa upset, when things are already so difficult without Papa having a regular job."

"My mother will be there with some other ladies, so it should be fine. Let's go."

Linna matched her pace to his as they walked along the sidewalk. Two men stood outside the Queen's Hotel, talking as they passed.

"Are you going to the Temperance meeting?" asked one, with a peal of laughter.

The other lifted his cap from his head, ran his fingers over the few grey hairs sticking up, and said, "Temperance all right. Those women would surely like to shut this town right down now, wouldn't they?"

Whispering to Henry, Linna asked, "What's temperance mean anyway?"

Henry, his voiced as hushed as hers had been, answered, "Temperance is about having no alcohol. Qu'Appelle has had a strong movement for that since the 1880s. It's all about something called Prohibition."

Linna wasn't a lot wiser after his explanation, but didn't want to question him further as they were nearly at the Town Hall. She decided she'd likely be able to figure it out from whatever was said at the meeting. At least, she thought, it didn't seem to have anything to do with the squatters. And, she reasoned, if lots of ladies were attending, she'd be able to tell Mama all about it, so she'd know what was happening.

Ladies, all dressed in their Sunday best, and the odd gentleman wearing a suit and tie, flocked into the Town Hall. A shiny black motorcar pulled up in front, and two men stepped out, dressed up the same. Linna looked down at her everyday dress and hoped she'd be able to disappear into a seat somewhere at the back, so she wouldn't feel so out of place.

Lagging behind the grown-ups, Henry and Linna examined the car with interest. Inside it had a pair of seats, one in the front and one in the back, made out of the softest light leather. A clock, even showing the right time, was set below the glass the driver peered through as he steered.

"Someday I'm going to drive a car," Henry said, reminding Linna of Konrad and his ever-changing dreams.

"I'll ride with you," she answered. "But I'd be too scared to ever drive one on my own. I don't even want a bicycle!"

"If I had a car," Henry added, "I could go exactly the

same places as everyone else, and at the same speed. I'd never be left behind."

Linna nodded.

The people on the sidewalk disappeared quickly, so Henry and Linna trudged up the outside stairs, then up the long flight that led to the second floor where they'd watched the rehearsal for the concert.

Henry's mother was at the door, helping get people seated, so she hurried them off to sit in a corner beside a pile of stage props still left from the concert. Linna thought she recognized the picture of the mountains she'd gazed at on that happy long-ago afternoon, before the mill burnt and everyone lost their jobs.

"Don't worry, Mother," Henry said. "We'll stay quiet back here, just listening."

Mrs. Spencer smiled. "I know you will."

Linna turned her attention to the two men settling in at the front of the room, who had driven up in the car.

Henry pointed. "That's J.K. McInnis, he's the editor of the *Regina Standard* newspaper. I've seen his picture before. The other man must be C.B. Keenleyside, who is the Secretary of the Temperance and Moral Reform Council."

None of the words, even their titles, made much sense to Linna.

As the local organizers were getting settled, Henry's mother sat in a chair at the rear. A tall lady peering over spectacles perched on her nose, stood and moved to the front of the room beside the two visitors.

She said, "Welcome, welcome everyone! We're so happy to have so many supporters out, to hear more about what the Christian Temperance Movement wants to do to improve the quality of life here in Qu'Appelle."

A fly buzzed over Linna's head, the sound as loud as a machine's hum in the stillness of the great room. Someone near the front sneezed, while someone else shuffled, making a chair screech as it inched across the floor. Linna leaned back, trying to disappear, and afraid to ask Henry any more questions. She'd just have to wait and see if she could figure it all out.

It didn't take very long. The ladies, she soon realized, were talking about the Qu'Appelle Liquor store that had just been closed, so her father couldn't buy any more lager there to have after his supper.

"What a wonderful move by the licence commissioner, wasn't it?" said a lady with a lilting voice that carried throughout the hall.

The question was met with a loud round of cheers and applause.

Linna was confused. What was wrong with lager? In Germany the monks at the monastery made the best lager, so surely there was nothing bad about lager. If there was, how could the monks make it?

The longer the meeting went on the more confused Linna became.

"Prohibition is the best thing for our town," said the lady looking over her spectacles, once the men had made their speeches. "Let's shut down all of the drinking establishments and make ours a community of Christian temperance! We have a motion to make the Town hold a plebiscite."

Again the room filled with cheers and hollering. Linna hadn't realized ladies in fancy dresses could be so loud.

Once the cheering ended a discussion period opened, and the room became a steady hum of voices. Linna listened intently to those around her, trying to piece everything together.

The people nearest her were two men who worked at the store. They didn't seem as keen on Christian temperance as the ladies next to them.

The man who usually weighed up her purchases said, "Good thing these women don't have the vote, isn't it?"

The other shook his head, answering, "Now that's for sure. Any decision making done by this town will go to all the men."

A lady she recognized as going to the French Mass, obviously overheard his comment and added, "And I suppose all the voters includes that community of squatters south of the tracks too. Isn't it bad enough they contribute just about no taxes to pay for the school we had to build to educate their children? Now they'll get to vote on Prohibition, too."

Linna felt herself turning red as she heard the word *squatters,* but she couldn't stop listening.

One of the men chuckled heartily and responded, "Now that's the truth, isn't it? Isn't likely a one of them will vote to get rid of lager in this town."

The lady, obviously upset with the way the discussion was going, burst out, "Well, if it's the squatter vote that swings this issue, then you can bet the Women's Christian Temperance Movement will see that the CPR finally does the right thing, and makes them get off the land."

Linna, unable to listen anymore, leaned over and whispered to Henry, "I have to go. My Mama is waiting for me to bring home some things."

Henry, his face serious, answered, "All right. I'll see you at the library on Thursday. I shouldn't have asked you to come."

Linna tried to smile. "I'm all right." She stood, trying to make herself as skinny and invisible as possible, and crept towards the door.

Sarah Booker stood right in the middle of the entrance, while her mama talked to another lady at the top of the stairs.

The only way out for Linna was to square her shoulders and walk right past.

Sarah glanced at her mother as Linna approached, then turned and whispered, "You go back to your side of the tracks, and tell everyone what's going to happen to you squatters."

Linna tried her best to ignore her, unable to even breathe until she was standing at the top of the stairs. Mrs. Booker never seemed to notice Sarah's comments or Linna's passing.

Outside, Linna's mind raced with what she'd heard. She turned towards the school, which sat right beside the Town Hall, dreading the day classes would start next week.

Kat was gone. Papa had no regular job, so there was little money for clothes or maybe even food. Now, the townspeople wanted to hold a vote...And Sarah's warning still rang in her ears. Where would they live if not in the soddie?

CHAPTER 10

Linna used her own hard-earned Saskatoon-picking money to buy the material for a new school dress, and to get her supplies.

Mama went with her to the dry goods store to pick them all out. *"Ich mag das am besten,"* Mama said, holding a piece of dark blue broadcloth up to her face.

Running her fingers over the soft, smooth material, Linna stared at the different bolts of fabric, trying to pick out one that would be pretty, and yet what Mama called *serviceable.* It wouldn't do to get a colour that would be dirty after only one or two days of wearing, but she was tired of always having blue.

"We could use little pearl buttons or make a big front collar and trim it with lace," Mama said, trying to be helpful.

Linna picked up yet another piece of material, to see what was underneath it. Then she saw it on another shelf, fabric the shade of a ripe red plum – not quite red and not quite purple.

Mrs. Buckley, who worked in the store, handed it to her. "That's one of our newest bolts of rayon. It's a good fabric that doesn't crease easily."

Linna thought immediately of Sarah, with her dresses always looking crisp and freshly ironed. "This is the one," she said immediately, pulling it out of the pile. "I shall have just a little round collar and some rows of embroidery along the front. Will you do it for me Mama? Your stitches are so much neater than mine!"

Mama nodded. "What colour embroidery? You'll need to pick some thread for that, too."

With the vision of what she wanted in her mind, it didn't take long for Linna to find exactly the shade she was looking for – one just a little darker than the fabric. She took some buttons to cover with the dress fabric, for a row down the back.

When Mrs. Buckley added up her choices, Linna was happy to find she still had fifty cents left of her summer earnings. Perhaps she'd save that for Christmas gifts, since she would be able to get books from the school library now instead of paying her money at the town library.

Konrad looked envious as he stared at the pile of things Linna assembled for her first day of school. Her pencils were sharpened, ready for writing words on the blank pages of her copybooks. She'd even had money for a fine quill pen and bottle of ink.

"I wish I could go to school," Konrad said, running his fingers over the skinny yellow pencils.

"Soon," Papa smiled, "soon, you'll be old enough for school."

"Play dominoes with me Linna." Konrad held out the box to her. "Let me count the dots."

While it always took so long for a game when Konrad counted, Linna agreed to play, dumping the box onto the rag rug, thinking sadly of Kat once more. She carefully counted out five dominoes for herself and five more for Konrad before turning one over in the middle. It had one dot on one end and four on the other.

"Let me, let me," roared Konrad, carefully touching each dot as he counted.

While he concentrated Linna listened to her parents.

Papa said, "There's to be a plebiscite in Qu'Appelle on selling spirits or lagers. The men here in the soddies will be allowed to vote."

Mama nodded. "Friar Bartholomew would shake his head to think of so much time and money spent on such a thing. What could be wrong with a stein of lager after a hard day's work?"

"I have it," Konrad announced, setting his domino up against the matching four dot one.

Linna didn't want to hear any more about the plebiscite, so turned her attention back to the game. She hadn't breathed a word to Mama or Papa about what she'd heard at the meeting, despite Sarah's warning.

Mama worked on the dress for the next four days, cutting, pinning, and tucking. Linna scurried around, trying to do all of the chores for her. It was important that she have the perfect new dress to begin in her new school. She sang bits of different *lieder* for Mama as she stitched, feeling her voice growing stronger the more she practised. Maybe someday she really could sing on stage like Mrs. Booker. The brave part of her wanted to ask Papa to take her along to talk to Mrs. Booker about singing, when he went on Monday nights to do their accounts, while the shy part was afraid to ask.

Finally it was the first day of school. Mama buttoned the back of her dress, and Linna ran her hands over the smooth front. It was perfect.

She set off for school at a leisurely pace. While there were a number of other boys and girls living in the soddies, both younger and older than her, no girls, as Kat had already told her, were the same age. The few older ones all seemed to have best friends already, so they walked in pairs or raced along to meet other children along the way.

Although it was still early, Henry waited outside on the school steps for Linna. "Hello," he shouted.

Linna raced the last few steps, feeling her syrup pail with its tomato sandwiches bang against her leg. It was much too far for children from the settlement to walk home at noon, then get back afterwards for classes, so she had a lunch to eat at school. "Hello, Henry," she said, suddenly breathless as she came to a stop.

The golden bricks of the school gleamed almost like a castle in the sunshine. It even had a pointed turret rising up the front wall into a point above an enclosed balcony.

"I'll show you where our classroom is," Henry said. "We can choose our seats."

Linna hoped fervently that the new teachers would let her stay in the same grade with Henry, even if she struggled for the first bit of the year with writing English. Surely her good skills at numbers would convince them to let her try the grade. "All right."

The new door didn't creak when it opened, or even groan, but admitted them to the smell of hardwood and paint.

"My first year of school I went to the old schoolhouse, until this one was built," said Henry, leading her proudly through its halls. "Now there's lots of room, even for the high school. We've had one for three years already. Someday I'll finish grade twelve here and then go on to university."

Linna hadn't thought about how far she wanted to go in school. Already many of the older children in the soddies had stopped attending.

Following Henry, Linna didn't have much time to peer into the rooms they passed, before they reached the wide staircase to the second storey. "We're up here." Henry pointed.

Grabbing the handrail, Linna enjoyed the feel of the smooth wood on her fingers. Her feet click-clacked on the hardwood, mixing with the corresponding sounds of a taller, heavier girl coming towards her. But there was lots of room for them to meet and pass.

It was exciting, being inside the bright new building. She had always enjoyed school before, and now that she could read English fairly well, was sure she could do well in Canada too.

"This room is for grade seven and eight together," said Henry, leading her into a big room at the top of the stairs. It was lined with green chalkboards on three walls, and long narrow windows on the fourth. The desks were laid out in rows so straight they might have been in ruler lines, drawn on the floor.

Several girls already there stared at Linna. Finally one said, "I like your dress. It's very pretty."

"Thank you," Linna said, surprised at the friendliness in the girl's voice. She didn't know what else to say, though, so simply followed Henry to the opposite side.

"I'm not very tall, so the teachers always make me sit near the front," Henry said. "Maybe you can sit behind me." He flopped down onto a golden bench seat attached to the front of a desk with iron scrolls along its side. She sat behind him, her desk attached to his seat. She wiggled the desk with her arms, grinning as he turned and their eyes met.

"I promise I won't wiggle you when you're writing," she said, "unless you'd rather have me in front of you."

Henry shrugged. "I think you've grown taller, so teacher would just move us."

Before she could answer, Linna heard Sarah Booker burst into the room. She didn't have to turn to see her face; she already knew her voice. As usual, a group of girls followed her.

"Oh Sarah," gushed the same girl who'd complimented Linna's dress, "you look so pretty today. I love your dress."

"My mother bought it for me in Regina," said Sarah, "when she took me to buy my school clothes. It's ready-made. I got two others, and new shoes too. You should see my new Sunday dress. It's beautiful." She stuck out her foot for the other girls to admire.

"You're so lucky Sarah."

"My mother only let me pick out one dress at the store. The dressmaker is doing my other ones," moaned the girl with a mole beside her nose.

"Linna," Sarah said, suddenly turning towards her. "Where do you go shopping south of the tracks?"

Several of the girls tried to cover their giggles with their hands.

Linna felt embarrassment flooding her. She could tell by the glances the other girls were giving one another, that they'd figured out pretty quickly Sarah didn't like her. It wasn't likely they'd be friendly anymore either.

"What difference does it make, Sarah?" interrupted Henry.

"I was just curious," Sarah said, pointedly turning back to her friends. "Have you picked your seats yet? I think I'll take the back again, maybe behind you Alice."

Alice, the tallest, appeared as happy as if she'd won a red ribbon. "That would be nice if teacher doesn't make you move!"

"Don't worry," Sarah replied, twirling one of her long blonde curls around her fingers. "They usually let me sit where I want."

Another swarm of students clattered up the stairs, chattering about all the things they'd done on their summer vacations. Several of them charged into the grade seven-eight room, dropping into back seats that weren't already taken. Two boys she recognized from the soddies took the empty ones behind Linna. At least they wouldn't taunt her.

Soon the room was full of students. A bell clanged to announce the beginning of classes, and Miss Jackson, the teacher, appeared in the doorway. She wasn't as heavy as Anke or as tall as Mama, but somewhere in between them both. With her brown hair drawn back tightly and pinned up, it was hard to guess her age. But Linna didn't care about those things. She only hoped for a teacher who would be patient while she learned English properly.

"Good morning class!"

The teacher's voice sounded warm and friendly. That was a good starting place. She continued, "I hope you've all come prepared to work hard this year, because there is a lot to..."

Adolph, the boy behind Linna, wiggled his desk as if he was already bored with school, making Linna's seat move. Catching herself quickly by bracing her feet on the floor, she accidentally kicked her lunch pail, so that it rolled out into the aisle.

Everyone in the classroom stopped looking at Miss Jackson and turned to stare at Linna. But the hardest stare to take was the one Miss Jackson turned on her.

"And who are you, young lady?" asked Miss Jackson. "Surely that belongs in the cloakroom, not under your desk."

Henry turned, mouthing the words, "I'm sorry," but Linna was on her own.

"Sorry, Miss Jackson, I didn't..." Linna faltered. Suddenly the English word for know disappeared from her head and she froze.

"Didn't what?" said the teacher.

Most of the class burst out laughing, although some tried to hide their grins.

"Know," mouthed Henry, turning once again.

"Know," said Linna, feeling so small she could fit through a mouse hole. "I'm Linna – Adeline – Mueller and this is my first day." She took a deep breath, and added, "I'm very s..s..sorry for disrupting your class."

Miss Jackson's expression softened. "Adeline Mueller?" she confirmed, running her finger through the register.

Linna nodded.

"I have you on my list. You may put everything but your books in the cloakroom." Miss Jackson pointed towards the door.

Linna rose, picked up her lunch pail and followed Miss Jackson's finger. Oh no! Sarah Booker's desk was the last one in the last row that sat right beside the cloakroom. Determined not to falter, Linna took one long step after another, until she was within reach of Sarah's seat. The only sounds were her shoes hitting the floor with each step. Every student's eyes seemed glued to her, waiting to see if she'd make another mistake they could laugh at.

Sarah stood and said, "I'll help her, Miss Jackson," in the sweet voice she saved for adults in authority.

Linna stopped abruptly. What was Sarah up to?

"Thank you, Sarah," said the teacher. "Go ahead Linna, what are you waiting for?"

Once again with no choice but to move forward, Linna followed Sarah into the long narrow cloakroom with its line of coat hooks and upper shelf. "Where?" she murmured.

Sarah's answer came out as a command. "Down there at the far end — and don't ever put anything next to this door, because that's where my things are going to go. I don't want yours anywhere near mine."

"Don't worry about that," Linna said, feeling a little calmer. She had to remember to do what Kat had told her, to stand up to Sarah. She walked slowly down the corridor. "And make sure nothing of yours ever ends up down here next to my things either."

When Linna emerged from the cloakroom the students were all focused on the blackboard where Miss Jackson was already writing down an assignment. It began, she saw, with words for grade sevens to spell. She gulped, slapping her hand over her mouth. The words were hard, very hard indeed.

The walk home after school was much slower than Linna's morning walk had been. Recesses at school hadn't been too bad, because Henry had shown her where everything was, and apologized five times at least for not telling her to put her lunch pail in the cloakroom. The boys behind her had smiled too, and been friendly. So had some of the younger children who met her on the playground, especially the ones who knew Konrad. It seemed he must be popular in the settlement by the way they all talked about him. She wished she'd fit in as well as he had.

At noon Henry had taken her to the school library, to show her all the books they had to choose from. It had eight tall shelves crammed full, at least double as many as the town library! He even helped her sign out an easy one so that she could practice her reading in English.

She stared into the sky of fluffy clouds. As Papa had promised, it was much cooler now, more like the weather in Germany. The dust from the harvest fields lay thick in the air without a wind to carry it away. She sneezed.

When she reached home, Linna burst through the door. "Mama," she said, not realizing the room was empty. Sudden disappointment swelled in her, and she struggled to keep tears from falling.

Instead of being cool and welcoming, the soddie was hot. A dozen jars of beans, canned from the garden, sat cooling on the table. The canner sat at the back of the stove. Linna wondered where they'd store these jars, since most of the spaces beneath the beds were already full of the first vegetables, and the fruits Mama had picked after Linna showed her where they grew. They had raspberries, black and red currants, and many saskatoons.

A second later Mama followed Konrad inside. "Was it good? What did you do?" asked Konrad, his grubby hands grabbing for the new books she still held.

Mama didn't say anything, but her eyes asked the same questions.

Linna handed Konrad the new book with pictures. He immediately dropped to the floor to open the pages carefully.

"School was all right. It will be hard, especially the English spelling words," Linna told them. "The numbers were easy. I am much better with my sums than anyone else." Indeed, even Sarah had made a remark – not a nice one – about Linna answering nearly all of the teacher's questions.

Mama gave her a hug. "That's good, Linna. And the other children, were they...friendly?"

"Some of them." Linna shrugged. "I missed having Kat, but she wouldn't have been in the same grade with me anyway." She would never tell Mama how mean Sarah was about things that Mama couldn't change.

"Your dress, was it all right?"

Linna nodded. "One of the older girls even said it was pretty."

When Papa came home she went through all of the details again, careful to tell him only the best parts of the day. Staring at her little brother, shooting marbles on the floor by himself, she added, "It sounds like everybody knows Konrad."

Mama nodded. "*Ja,* I must always hunt for him. You never know where he'll be playing."

"But I like to play." Konrad looked up. "And I have lots of children to play with here. Way more than in Nana's village."

Linna worked up her courage to ask Papa a question. "And what did you do all day, Papa?" As mean as Sarah was, she was always nice around grown-ups, so perhaps if Linna could get Papa to take her with him to the Bookers', she might learn more about becoming a singer in Canada.

Papa sighed. "Hammered nails in a new house going up on the far side of town. There's enough work to keep me busy for the rest of this week..."

Although he didn't add the rest of the words, Linna knew he meant he had nothing to do for the week after.

"Are you going to the Bookers' tonight, Papa?" she asked anxiously.

Papa shook his head. "No, Jack has gone to Winnipeg on business. It will be a week or so before he returns. He's following up on something I advised, and expects he'll make quite a lot of money on the deal."

Linna felt both disappointment and relief, although for Papa she knew it meant no money for awhile longer. She wondered if there was some way Mr. Booker would share the money he made with Papa.

Mama squeezed Papa's shoulder and took his hand. "Maybe someone will ask you to help with the harvest."

"Maybe," Papa sighed. "Maybe they will."

CHAPTER 11

Linna loved the slow days of fall, which were so much cooler than the summer had been. Beyond the settlement the harvest equipment rumbled through the day and into the night, cutting down the crops. At school she felt almost invisible, at least where Sarah was concerned. While Henry did his best to make her feel welcome, she still missed Kat and wished she had a girl for a friend. At night she studied and studied and studied, on word after word after word, until she could spell them correctly.

Papa got a job on one of the threshing crews, working with the sheaves of grain, so Mama seemed happier. At night, when he came home, it was usually dark already, so there was little time for anyone to talk.

One Friday, his face weary and tired, he said, "Linna, there's only me and Adolph Schmidt to keep ahead of the two binders with stooking. His two boys work on the crew, and one's younger than you. Do you want to come as well? You'll get a half-day's pay, same as the boys."

It didn't take long for Linna to decide. "Yes, Papa!"

"You'll need to be up before dawn then, because the hayrack arrives to take us to the field at daybreak."

Linna was already used to her father's early hours, although she usually pulled the quilts over her face and drifted back off to sleep. But she knew Mama rose, lit the fire, and made a steaming pot of porridge for Papa no matter how early it was.

Hardy able to sleep a wink, Linna nestled under her covers, waiting for morning. She was excited about working at harvest. She'd already helped Mama can so many beans she felt like she just might get skinnier and turn green. Surely stooking would be more fun. And she would earn real pay!

The next morning, shivering in the chill outside air, even with the hot oatmeal on her insides, Linna watched the eastern sky grow light. Without even thinking, she began to hum a little song. Papa nodded and smiled.

Half a dozen men and two boys were already on the hayrack when it arrived, pulled by a team of prancing black horses. Papa helped her up on the rack, then jumped on with the five other men who stood waiting. It felt even cooler as the horses began trotting along at a brisk pace, so she was glad of the jacket Mama had made her bring.

While she didn't want to stare at anyone, Linna let her eyes wander over the crew. They all seemed strong, from the grey-bearded man, on down to boys her age. Their faces didn't look like they often smiled, or ever thought of having fun. It made her shudder to think that Papa was one of them now. What of his dreams to return to banking, to work with his mind, not his hands?

The shorter of the boys, his brown hair clipped up around his ears, leaned over and said, "Have you ever been stooking?"

Linna shook her head. She stood shyly near Papa, realizing how much taller she had grown over summer, since she came nearly to his shoulder already. Mama spent time every night letting down hems and sewing to get all of their clothes ready for the coming winter.

The boy grinned and said, "We can work together if you like. Fred, he's my brother, is big enough to do it alone."

Papa nodded. "That's a good idea, Paul."

The hayrack lurched as it bounced over a rough piece of ground, and Linna grabbed the weathered crossbraces at the front for balance. "I'm Linna. I'll try to learn quickly."

Paul nodded, but said nothing more, turning his attention to the conversation of his father and the men around him.

Soon the hayrack slowed and stopped. "First field," shouted the man driving the horses.

"We'll get off here," said Paul, dropping easily to the ground.

Linna looked at Papa, but he said nothing, so she gingerly sat and stuck her legs over the edge of the rack.

"Jump," said Paul, so she did, her feet hitting the solid ground and taking two steps forward on their own, as if they wanted to run away with her.

Golden bundles of grain tied in the middle by the binder, lay scattered across the field for as far as Linna could see. Before she might object, Papa shouted, "I'll see you at dinnertime," and the hayrack rattled away.

The sun had risen during the ride, so the field glowed like gold spread out over the soil. In many ways, she realized, it was gold: gold to the farmer who could pay his bills, gold to the worker who helped to harvest it, gold to the hungry people who would eat the bread.

Paul gestured at the stooks lying on top of what remained of the wheat stalks. "This one looks pretty good, so we'll take it first."

Linna stared at it, comparing it to the nearest other one. "What's the difference?"

"Better shape. Even." Paul grabbed it. "Get that one behind you, it's good too."

Doing as she was instructed, Linna picked up the sheaf in her arms. She'd already figured out from seeing the stook piles in other fields that the sheaves had to be stood upright and leaned together in piles, so she quickly moved forward and set it opposite Paul's sheaf.

"Good. Now gather up some more and lean 'em in. We need eight or ten to a stook."

The next one Linna grabbed was loose, its string gone. She gathered it up carefully, and asked, "What about this one? It's broken."

"Goes against the others with a good one overtop."

Sheaf after sheaf Linna leaned the bundles into one another. Her legs itched through the long stockings Mama had made her wear. Her arms itched from the grain. Even her eyes itched from the dust that filled them as she worked.

She soon found there was no sense trying to talk to Paul as they stooked. He bent down, picked up a sheaf, stacked it; bent down, picked up a sheaf, stacked it. So she followed his lead, leaning her sheaf in wherever he gestured, hurrying to cover any loose ones with a well-tied, strong one. Her throat grew dry, and she stopped to take a sip from the small jug of water Mama had tied around her waist. Overhead the sun climbed higher and higher into the sky, until she guessed it was mealtime. Her stomach growled angrily with hunger.

At what she guessed to be noon, the hayrack appeared on the horizon to pick them up, and she gladly crawled up and flopped onto it, too weary to stand. She gazed out at the rows and rows of stooks and felt pride in her morning's work.

"You're pretty good," Paul said. "I'm fast and you kept up."

Linna soaked up the compliment like it was syrup over a pancake, and smiled. "I sure am hungry though."

"Just wait until you see dinner! Mrs. Whittingham, she's a good cook."

"Do you go to school?" asked Linna, pleased that Paul was finally ready to talk. "I've never seen you or your brother."

Paul shrugged. "I may go back after harvest. Fred's finished fourth grade, so he's done all he's gonna do. We don't go to town school, though, we go to Grassmere up to grade eight."

"Oh," Linna said. "What grade are you in?"

"Second," he answered. "I can read, so that's pretty good. Don't need much more."

"How old are you?"

"Nine, going on ten. I'm going to get my own farm someday," he added, his eyes glowing with excitement.

Linna thought of all the things she learned in books, and how much she enjoyed the challenges of doing more numbers. School was fun, even if Sarah made sure none of the girls wanted to be her friend. She still had Henry. Walking back and forth she had the younger children from the settlement to laugh and talk with, and she helped them learn new English words. Yes, she decided, going to school was a good thing for her.

Seeing how sure Paul was of what he wanted to do, though, Linna answered, "I bet you'll have a good farm."

The first thing she wanted when they arrived at the farmhouse was a big cold drink of water, to wash the dust out of her throat. She stood in line behind the men at the well and water trough, splashing cold water on her face, then lifting her freshly filled water jug to her lips.

The threshing crew laughed and joked, so it sounded like a celebration instead of a workday to Linna. They didn't look at all like the quiet men who had ridden on the hayrack at dawn. It could have been the fair all over again, except her muscles were beginning to stiffen up already from all the work.

Dinner was as good as Paul had predicted: fried chicken, roast ham, potatoes with dill, bean pickles, beetroot pickles, turnips, carrots, and three kinds of pie. Linna couldn't decide which one to have, so Mrs. Whittingham gave her a small piece of lemon meringue and a small one of pumpkin. It was the best dessert she'd ever eaten.

By dark, when the hayrack dropped her and Papa off at home, she was much too tired to do anything but fall into her bed. Tomorrow was Sunday, and the crew had a day of rest, so she was done her job. She added the shiny new fifty-cent piece she received for wages to the money already in her tiny cup, and drifted off to sleep.

The next day she and Papa joked with one another about things that had happened with the threshing crew.

It felt good to have something just between the two of them. Working so hard for just one day made her see how difficult it must have been for him to leave his accounts to work as a labourer instead. As they laughed it almost felt like the old days, back in Germany. At church that night she gave thanks, and sang with all her heart.

September disappeared and October followed. Harvest finished and Papa no longer had work to go to everyday. He went from business to business, looking for anything that he could do, but all he found were jobs that lasted for a day or two, and a few more part-days of doing accounts for businesses.

In the German community everyone was a little sad as the time for Oktoberfest came and went without the annual celebration and feasting. There were no tents, no monks or brewers with their lager, no sausages, no roast chicken, no fish, no giant pretzels, no red gingerbread hearts. Before they left Germany in June, everyone had already been planning the biggest Oktoberfest ever for the one-hundredth anniversary – it had been a century since Crown Prince Ludwig and Princess Therese held the first one to celebrate their marriage. Instead, the men had lager and horseshoes, while the women and children picnicked nearby on a warm October Sunday afternoon. Linna helped Mama and Anke with the boys, missing Kat and thinking how strange it felt to have everyone speaking German around her once again.

The Saskatchewan prairie put on its best set of clothes for fall. Leaves turned glorious shades of red, brown, and yellow before they withered and fell to the ground. Everything else was golden, from the never-ending wheat and oat fields, to the sunset that came earlier every night. In the morning frost turned the rooftops to white, and Linna thought of the cold and snows Papa promised would soon arrive.

Now that he had so many days he didn't work, Papa did the accounts for the Bookers during the day instead of on Monday nights. Linna was disappointed, because it meant she had no way to see if Mrs. Booker could help her with her singing, but she was happy Papa could be home with them after dark.

One Monday, on her way home from school, Linna stopped at the Post Office as she always did. "Any mail for the Mueller's?"

Much to her surprise, the Postmaster handed her a crumpled letter. "Looks like another letter from Germany," he said.

"Mama will be so happy." Linna ran her fingers over the neat square printing, almost as if she could touch the hand that had written it.

She tucked the letter between the pages of her spelling book and hurried off down the road towards home. Her mind filled with thoughts of the many things that could have happened since the last letter: perhaps Nana had recovered and needed her; maybe Tante

Karoline wanted her to come back and help with things; maybe...Linna stopped. She wasn't sure she'd really want to return to Germany even if they asked, although it would be easier for Papa to feed them if there was one less. For a second she thought how nice it would be to have her aunts and uncles and cousins all around to help when there were problems, like they had been in Germany. In Canada the four of them just had each other.

"Mama, Mama," she shouted, as she rushed into the house. "There's a letter!"

Mama dropped the beetroot she was peeling into the kettle, and tried to squeeze the purple juice from her hands back into the pot. "Read it to me, Linna."

Linna carefully opened the top of the letter, trying not to rush so she wouldn't tear anything important. She read:

Dear Karl, Frieda, Linna and Konrad:

My wedding was wonderful. I missed you all being here for it. I am happy with Adolph and his family.

Nana was able to come to the wedding, but she closed her eyes for the last time a few days after. I miss her. We buried her in the churchyard with all the family who have already gone.

Helmut's family has grown again with the birth of twins this fall. They are both big healthy boys, but they keep everyone very busy.

I hope you are all well. I may not write often, as I no longer have my own money for the postage and my time is full with taking care of Adolph's mother, since she is unable to leave her bed. But I will think of you all the time. Elli sends her love, but she is busy with school and I don't see her often anymore, so there is no letter from her.

With love always,
Karoline

Linna stared down at the neatly printed words. Why had her aunt left the castle where she was so happy, to marry Adolph, anyway? Linna realized, sadly, that the home she remembered in Germany was entirely gone.

"Poor Papa," whispered Mama. "He will feel badly that he wasn't there to say goodbye to Nana."

Linna wrapped her arms around Mama, feeling guilty that she had not thought first about Papa losing his own mother. "Nana was so proud Papa came to Canada." The words made her feel better as she knew they would comfort Papa, too.

But that wasn't all of the bad news for the day. When Papa came home he told them what he'd heard while doing the accounts for the Bookers. "The liquor plebiscite didn't pass, and the women went to the CPR. They have sold this land to a real estate agent named Mr. Leet. It sounds like he plans to make all thirty-four families here move, or make arrangements to pay him rent."

"What are we going to do?" Linna asked, her heart full of fear for the future.

"I don't know," Papa said quietly. "I have my name in at a few places, but I don't know if things will happen quickly enough."

Linna didn't ask quickly enough for what. Instead, she took out the dominoes to play with Konrad and keep him quiet. Mama removed a loaf of fresh bread from the oven, to slice it hot for their supper of bread and venison. Luckily, Anke's husband had good luck with hunting, and they had shared the meat.

That night Papa was silent after he read Tante Karoline's letter. He sat at the table, running his fingers over the pages of the big German bible they'd brought from home, reading passage after passage. Linna wished she could just put her arms around him and hug him, but somehow she still couldn't. Instead she crawled onto her bed and sang hymns softly, watching as the weariness eased on his face.

The next day, the temperature shot up so high Linna had to shed her fall sweater. "I thought fall was supposed to be cool," she said to Henry, as she sat on the school steps studying another list of spelling words. While she sometimes got most of them correct, not once had she ever got a hundred percent, even with all of her efforts. Sometimes she felt like giving up completely on learning to be good at English, both spelling it and getting the words right. So many words were confusing when she saw them on paper – like *to, too,* and *two.* Why did there need to be so many?

"My father calls this warm October weather Indian Summer," Henry said. "We'll likely get winter soon after it ends."

"Is it really as cold in winter as Papa says?" Linna thought of the small box of coal they used to keep warm now, and how much money it cost to fill.

Henry nodded. "Sometimes. Some days the sun shines and the kids go skating on the ice rink we make behind the schoolyard." His face held the sadness it always did when he told Linna about the things he couldn't do.

"I don't think I shall skate," said Linna firmly, partly because she knew her family wouldn't have money to buy such a thing as skates, and partly because she wanted to make sure Henry wasn't left all alone.

"What will happen now," Henry continued slowly, "to your family...now that the CPR have sold the land?"

Tears suddenly filled her eyes, and her throat felt tickly and full, as if she'd swallowed a frog. She just shook her head, and tried to concentrate on her spelling words.

Sarah and her group of friends sauntered past Linna, pretending as usual that they didn't see her. Linna pretended she didn't see them right back. However, she had a harder time not hearing them. If only one of the other girls would be her friend, she would feel better.

Henry gazed out at the schoolyard, where the other children played tag, squealing and racing after one another. "I hope something good will happen for your family, Linna."

Linna wiped her eyes, determined not to cry in front of the other children, especially Sarah. If Henry could manage to smile and laugh while he sat on the sidelines yearning to be like other kids, surely she could manage as well.

Sarah stopped abruptly, only a little ways from them. "My Mama says it won't be long before the squatters all have to move," she said. "There are big things happening in town, even if the liquor plebiscite didn't pass."

Linna ignored her, but Henry asked, "What kind of big things?"

Sarah shrugged, a secret little smile on her face. "Business ventures, and my father is on one of the new boards."

Thwack! Linna closed her book. She didn't really want to hear anymore about Sarah or the businesses her father was in. It didn't seem fair that her father did all of Mr. Booker's accounts, but nobody acknowledged his part. Surely they would miss his skills if he were forced to move somewhere else? But the somewhere was the big problem for Linna. Where would they be without the soddie? It seemed like life in Canada was not what any of them had hoped for, not Papa, not her, that was for sure. But now there was no way to go back to Germany either. What could they do?

When Monday, October 31st arrived, Linna went along to church to give thanks for the abundance of the harvest along with all other Canadians, since it was proclaimed a National Day of Celebration. Although it was a day for thanksgiving, Linna wondered how many other people worried what would happen when winter came.

CHAPTER 12

Linna wiggled in her bed, snuggling further down into the covers. A strange, eerie whistling seemed to be coming in around the door and window frames. She poked a finger out to find that it was as cold inside as it usually was outside.

Papa stood at the big black stove, coaxing some flames from a few sticks of wood. The box of coal beside the stove was nearly empty. He had no work lined up for the week, so they were burning as little as possible and let the fire go out at night. He turned to Linna and said, "Stay in bed for a while yet until it warms some. The temperature is way below freezing this morning."

Crack-crack. Mama broke the thin layer of ice on the water pail, dipping out a pot of water for breakfast. "It will warm up quick and we'll have breakfast."

Linna didn't argue, but closed her eyes thinking of the frigid walk to school. She guessed winter in Canada had truly begun. Everyone had told her it was a very warm fall, but sooner or later the season would change.

The first thing Miss Jackson did at school that morning was announce it was time to begin preparations for the Christmas concert. "I've chosen a play that needs eleven students to act, so we'll also have a choir of six girls for the singing that goes with it. That leaves four of you to build the sets, change them on performance night, and do the prompts for the actors on stage."

Excitement surged through Linna. Singing! There was going to be a choir.

Henry turned and whispered, "Make sure you volunteer for the choir, no matter what happens."

Linna nodded, wondering what could possibly occur that would make her not want to sing, but she soon found out.

Sarah stood, pasting her best smile on her face. "Miss Jackson, my mother does all of the work for the annual summer concert, so I know exactly how things should go. I'd like to direct the choir. I've had voice lessons, so I can pick the best singers, and see to it they do a good job of all the songs."

"My goodness, Sarah," said Miss Jackson, "that's a pretty big job for a grade seven student."

"I can do it," Sarah replied with assurance. "My mother's a very good organizer, and so am I."

"Well, as long as none of the older girls really wants the job, I guess it's yours, Sarah. Girls," said Miss Jackson, "does anyone else want to be in charge of the choir?"

Linna surveyed the room anxiously, hoping anyone else but Sarah would volunteer. Nobody did.

"Well Sarah, I guess you are the director. I thought we'd decide on the choir and cast the play parts this morning, so let's go ahead. Girls, who wants to be in the choir?"

Henry turned again, but Linna's hand was already in the air. She smiled at him. Even Sarah Booker couldn't keep her from doing this!

Four of Sarah's friends put up their hands too, but Sarah said, "Nelda Fessant, your singing sounds all squawky, like you're a Mallard duck instead of a song-bird."

Everyone in the class burst out laughing, while Nelda's face turned all red.

"Sarah," Miss Jackson said quickly, "perhaps we should have singing tryouts."

It didn't appear to Linna from the expression on Sarah's face like that was exactly what she'd had in mind, but Sarah always seemed to know when it was wise to agree with her elders. "All right. We'll have to do it now though, won't we, so the leftovers can go in the play."

"They won't be *leftovers* Sarah, they'll be the actors and actresses," Miss Jackson said, smiling encouragement at the other students.

It seemed to Linna that no matter what Sarah said this morning she seemed to be hurting somebody's feelings. But, Linna decided, today was the day Sarah Booker was not going to pretend Linna was invisible anymore – not where there was singing involved. She couldn't help Papa get a job. She couldn't help Mama manage with very little money. But she could make her dreams of singing come true in Canada.

Miss Jackson continued, "So, girls, I'll sit down at the piano and play a little of a Christmas song you know and you'll each have a turn singing. Then we'll pick the choir. Boys, I'd like you all to go up to the library for the next fifteen minutes to exchange your library books, so your time is well spent while we're doing this."

Linna watched the boys leave, guessing the real reason was so they wouldn't laugh at the girls trying to sing while they were all being stared at. She wished Henry had been allowed to stay. He would have given her confidence.

The singing tryouts went up and down the rows of desks, starting at the very back with Sarah. Her voice, as Linna expected, was strong and clear, just like her mother's had been at the concert rehearsal. Linna wished she could take voice lessons too. If only she could visit Mrs. Booker and talk to her about lessons, she'd feel better. She sang her *lieder* every day, but maybe that wasn't enough.

Some of the girls were nervous and their voices cracked a little, but all of them tried, even Nelda. While Linna would never have said it herself, Nelda's voice did sound a little like a duck's.

Linna was the very last one to have a turn, and there were already at least six nice voices to choose from, so she was sure that Sarah would not pick her.

Standing, Linna walked to Miss Jackson instead of staying beside her desk as the others had done, and whispered, "I don't know all the words to any English Christmas carols, so I'll have to read them from your music book while you play."

Miss Jackson whispered back, "That will make it very difficult for you dear, perhaps you'd rather wait until you study some of them."

Glancing back at Sarah, Linna knew this was her only chance to join the choir. "No," she said, "I'll try it now. I'd like to sing the same one Sarah did. Was it 'Silent Night?'" She had considered just singing the German words when she recognized *"Stille Nacht! Heilige Nacht,"* but decided Sarah might use that as an excuse to keep her out.

"That's a good choice," said Miss Jackson. "Several of the girls have sung that, so you'll have a good idea how it goes."

As Miss Jackson put her fingers on the keys Linna tried to make herself relax, so she could feel happy enough to bring the music in her heart to life. She thought of the wide open prairie where she'd sung for Kat, and the times she'd sung for her family, then opened her mouth and let the words flow, filling the classroom with sound.

When she finished nobody said a word. She walked back to her desk, the clip-clop of her shoes echoing through the room.

One of the boys opened the door and poked his head inside. "Done yet, teacher? We've all picked new books."

"Yes," Miss Jackson said. "You may tell the others to return to class now so we can choose the parts for the play." The boy closed the door again, and the teacher turned to the girls.

Before Miss Jackson could continue, Sarah leapt to her feet beside her desk and surveyed the girls in the room. "I think I'll..."

Linna didn't think at all; she just knew she wouldn't let Sarah keep her from making her dream happen! She jumped to her feet.

Standing speechless for a second, Linna stared at Sarah. She took a deep breath, finding her courage slowly. "I want you to know...I also have experience singing. At Castle Colmberg I heard the very famous opera singer, Gisela Staudigl, perform some of Brangäne's songs from *Tristan and Isolde...*"

Miss Jackson interrupted, "Goodness, Linna, you've certainly heard one of the best!"

While Sarah stood still as solid rock, some of the girls gasped and their eyes widened with amazement. The room was so quiet Linna could hear her heart thumping.

"What was it like?" asked Eunice, breaking the silence.

Straightening her shoulders, Linna answered, "It was wonderful. She sang like an angel, and her dress was as fine as any Queen's, or finer."

"I wish I could have the chance to be inside a castle or to see a famous opera singer," Nelda said, smiling directly at Linna.

A flush of crimson moved up Sarah's face. "I don't see what difference it makes who you've seen."

Linna took another deep breath. She knew what she wanted, and she was going to do everything she could to get it. "I have been singing the same *lieder* as she does, daily, for over a year, and I can do parts from the opera as well."

"That's lovely, Linna," said Miss Jackson. "You're going to have to tell us more about Germany. It sounds like you have many interesting stories."

Everyone in the room turned to look at Sarah, who stood, hands clenched into fists at her sides, staring right back at Linna.

"I don't mind if Sarah directs the choir," Linna said. "I just want to sing in it." She didn't back down, not a bit.

Sarah slowly surveyed the room. "Well, you were on my list anyway, so it doesn't really matter who you've seen or what you sing for practice. I also want Ruth, Annie, Eunice, and Vera. But since I'm in charge you all have to know that if you don't sing well, or learn all of the words, or follow my directions, you will be out." With her last words her eyes met Linna's, an equally determined expression on her face.

Miss Jackson cleared her throat. "Well, girls, I guess that sounds like everything is organized."

Linna slapped her hand over her mouth to keep from shouting with joy. She had done it! She had faced Sarah Booker down. She was in the Christmas choir!

The rest of the day Linna could not think or talk about anything else. Henry seemed to understand and just listened. After school she almost danced all the way home down the snow-packed road to the settlement. "Mama, Mama, I'm in the choir!" she shouted, opening the door.

Mama dropped her sewing needle and the old coat she was taking apart. She leapt to her feet, crossed the room in two strides, and threw her arms around Linna. "*Wonderbar! Ja,* you are a singer Linna. I am proud of you."

Linna hugged Mama back, then set her precious music book, with all the words and music for the songs she'd be singing at the Christmas concert, on the table. Konrad picked it up to look, but dropped it quickly when he saw there were no pictures.

Papa arrived home just before dark to share in the celebration. Linna lit the coal oil lamp and some candles to brighten the room, then helped Mama finish making a special meal. As Linna worked, she sang, and sang, and sang until Konrad put his hands over his ears.

Papa laughed, and said, "Let's hear some more!"

Linna began again, *"Stille nacht, heilige nacht,"* singing the German words instead of the English "Silent Night."

Supper began with sauerkraut soup, one of Linna's favourite things. Mama had made a big crock full of enough sauerkraut to last the winter, from the cabbages in the garden. Linna, unable to resist, often stuck her hand into the salty brine and pulled out a handful to eat after school.

After the soup came *weiner schnitzel,* made with venison instead of veal, and *spatzle,* the tiny dumplings that were the first things Linna ever learned how to cook on her own. For dessert they had *apfelstrudel,* a rare treat in Canada, since there weren't as many apples in Qu'Appelle as there had been in Germany. But Mama had run all over the settlement and borrowed two in order to celebrate Linna's special day.

Linna took the last bite of *apfelstrudel,* thinking it was the best she'd ever tasted. "Mama," she said, "thank you for making me such a nice supper." She hadn't even told Mama about standing up to Sarah at school, although she was celebrating that as much as getting into the choir.

"It was good," said Konrad. "Can you play marbles with me now Papa? Can you?"

"This is Linna's night," Papa said. "Let's see what she wants to do."

Linna stared around her home, toasty warm after having the stove hot to cook the supper. "I just want to help Mama with the dishes, then maybe have her brush my hair while we watch you and Konrad play, Papa. Is that all right?"

Mama nodded. "*Ja,* that's good."

Papa reached across and squeezed her hand. "That sounds like a nice way to spend the evening."

The next morning Linna awoke to the howl of the wind. While she waited for the room to warm up so she could jump out of bed for breakfast, white flakes of snow fell behind Papa as he closed the door on his return from the outhouse.

Papa hung his coat, and said, "Perhaps you should stay home from school today Linna. You've never felt a prairie wind when it is so cold, or the snow is falling."

Linna would not consider staying home! She had things to learn and the first choir practice to attend. So after breakfast she got ready to walk the long way into town and school.

"You must dress warmly today," Mama said, making her pull on a pair of lined pants over her long stockings. "They will keep your legs from freezing."

"But Mama," Linna groaned. "None of the girls who live in town wear these!"

Mama shook her head. "It doesn't matter. The other girls from here must do the same."

Reluctantly Linna did up the pants underneath her skirt. Perhaps if she took them off quickly at school nobody would notice, since her overcoat went way below her knees anyway. She pulled the hood of her navy coat up, and wrapped a bright red scarf over her nose and around her neck. By the time she went outside, her eyes were the only part not covered.

There were very few children walking to school this morning, so Linna stayed alone behind a group of three older boys making zigzag footprints in the snow. The first part of the way, through the settlement, was not too bad. But once the soddies were no longer around them to block the wind, she felt its bite right through her many layers of clothing. She wiggled her fingers in their mittens, pulling one hand into the long arms of her coat to keep it warm, while carrying her books and lunch in the other.

"Let's hurry!" shouted one of the boys.

"It's too cold out here!" gasped another, as they all rushed ahead.

Linna, feeling cold seep through her leather shoes to her toes, did the same. Hurrying down the road, she passed the railroad tracks and the rubble of the mill. With each second she was sure the wind grew stronger, until it seemed to howl louder than a coyote.

It chased her down the street, until she turned another corner. Then, instead of hitting her back, it hurled the icy snow against the side of her face, finding spaces the scarf didn't cover. She wondered if she would freeze to death before she got there.

Finally she reached the school. Her fingers ached from the cold, and she could barely feel her toes at all. She was sure tears, if she had cried, would have turned to icicles on her cheeks.

"Oh my goodness, you must be nearly frozen," Miss Jackson exclaimed, as Linna burst through the entrance into the warmth.

Not sure she could speak, Linna nodded.

Miss Jackson took the end of her scarf, and started unwrapping her face. "Give me your things, and come warm up by a radiator. How wise you are to have those pants on!"

Linna obediently removed mittens and coat, moving to the hissing radiator in one of the first-floor class-rooms with her. The radiator sputtered and banged, but heat eventually came as well. Through the long, narrow windows above the radiator she saw snow hurtle by, and wind snuck in around the window frames, even though the school was almost brand new.

Miss Jackson said, "You stay here until you're warmed through and through. I must go back to supervise students coming in." She hurried away, her long black skirt swirling around her black stockings and shoes.

As Linna's hands and toes started to warm, they tingled so painfully she felt tears threatening. The only thing that stopped them was Henry coming into the room.

"Why did you come to school today?" he asked. "It is so bitter with the wind and snow you should have stayed home."

Teeth chattering, Linna answered, "I couldn't give Sarah any reason to take me out of the choir."

Henry's face was serious. "I've known her since we were small, and I don't think she would do that. She can be very nice."

"Yes," muttered Linna, "just not to squatters."

"No, it's not really that," said Henry. "Her mother wants her to be a lady like her relatives in England, so she's never allowed to have any fun at all. She has to talk correctly. She has to act properly. She has to be best at everything."

As Linna thought about it, she realized it must be true. Sarah never seemed to be allowed to do ordinary things like the other children. Why, her mama had even been upset she didn't get the red ribbon in the girls' race on fair day. Maybe sometimes Sarah wished she could be somebody else too.

"Well," said Linna. "Maybe the choir will be wonderful and will make her mother proud." For a second Linna wondered if her singing would be good enough for Mrs. Booker.

Miss Jackson hurried back into the room, with little boys hanging on to each of her hands. "I'm going to find someone to take all of you back to the settlement after school today, unless this wind goes down," promised Miss Jackson.

"Thank you," Linna said, with relief.

Indeed, many children didn't make it to school at all that day, including half of the choir, so there was no meeting or practice at noon at all. Miss Jackson, true to her word, had the principal take his team and wagon home with the children. When Linna walked through the door she said, "Oh Mama, I hope winter won't be like this every day! It is terrible outside. Miss Jackson arranged a ride home for all of us."

"What a nice lady," said Mama. "*Ja,* it's a very nasty day. Mr. Booker came for your father with his wagon early this afternoon, and he isn't home yet. I hope he also gets a ride back."

Mama, Linna, and Konrad waited and waited and waited. They didn't want to eat without Papa. Soon it grew darker, even though they couldn't see the sun setting through the heavy clouds. The wind sounded stronger, angrier, and uglier.

Finally, the door creaked and Papa stepped inside with a blast of cold night air. His face, though, didn't look at all like Linna expected. In three long steps, he crossed the room, grabbed Mama up into his arms and pretended to dance her around.

"Sing for us, Linna!" he cried, thumping his foot on the floor, throwing snow around the room like a dog shakes water.

"What, what is it?" murmured Mama, holding him still in the middle of the tiny room. "What are we singing for?"

Papa's eyes glowed, as he lifted Konrad up from where he stood like he was still a baby, and tossed him towards the ceiling, when Mama wouldn't dance. "Because I have a new job – the kind of job I came to Canada to find! I'm going to be a banker again. One of the men has transferred to Winnipeg, so there's finally an opening for me at the Royal Bank. Jack Booker took me down and personally recommended me, so that's how I got on."

At the words, Mama threw her arms around Linna, dragging Papa and Konrad into her hug too. In a moment, Mama glanced back at the supper she'd been tending carefully, and stopped.

Mama said, "Our supper's almost ruined!"

"It will still be wonderful," Papa said, "because it's another celebration supper."

"You mean it's a leftover celebration supper from last night," Mama said, laughing.

"Yes, we have lots to celebrate."

Once the food was all served into plates, Mama asked, "But what about the real estate man? Are we going to pay him rent money to stay here?"

Papa smiled. "No, that's what kept me so long at the bank. As an employee I can have a good loan, so we can build our own house right in town. Jack Booker agreed to sign to guarantee it as well, since I'm new." He turned to Linna, "It's going to be small to start. There'll only be a big room and two little bedrooms on the first floor, and an attic room for Linna above."

Linna dropped her fork, so it rattled in her plate. She looked around at the soddie wondering exactly when it had begun to feel like home, so that now, thinking about getting a real house, it felt like moving and giving something up again.

"When," Mama whispered, "when can we get this house?"

"I think I can get enough help that it can be done before Christmas, if there's another warm spell. Quite a few of the other families here are buying land from the town and moving to the East side, so we'll all help each other build. Ours will be one of the first. Most won't go up until spring when the men get work."

"Can it really be?" asked Mama. "Can everything change with the blink of an eye?"

"When dreams come true, they can," Papa said, scooping the last of the *spatzle* onto his plate.

"How do you make dreams come true?" asked Konrad, his small voice serious.

"With hard work," Mama said, setting a small bowl

of saskatoon berries beside his plate. "It always takes hard work and determination."

Thoughts of a house in town ran through Linna's mind as she tried to go to sleep. A two-storey house so close to school it would only take her ten minutes to get there, and near Henry's house, so they could study together after school. She would be able to go every day without fearing she'd freeze, like this morning. But when she closed her eyes, her own dream filled her mind, the dream of singing on the big stage. It would be in the Town Hall, on the same stage where she'd heard Mrs. Booker sing, but the room would be full of Christmas decorations, not the set for the play. Miss Jackson would give her a note on the piano and the choir would start. She'd look out at the crowd and know Papa and Mama and Konrad were all watching and listening as she, Adeline Mueller, opened her mouth and sang.

CHAPTER 13

The first choir practice was at noon hour the next day. Linna quickly ate her piece of bread and syrup, then went to the only place left in school for them to practise – the back staircase to the second floor. Miss Jackson sat in front of the piano, and Sarah took up a place on the first stair, near her. Eunice, a grade eight girl who towered over the boys, quickly hurried up to the top stair, no doubt before anyone else could complain they couldn't see over her or sing around her. Anxious to get next to her, Linna rushed up the stairs.

"You have a pretty voice," whispered Eunice, as they both opened their songbooks.

"Thank you," Linna whispered back. "So do you."

While Miss Jackson was warming up at the piano, Sarah turned to face her group. "We're going to be the best choir ever heard in Qu'Appelle School, so you'll need to be practising day and night." She narrowed her eyes at Linna. "Everyone will have to know all the words off by heart."

"Okay girls," Miss Jackson said. "Let's begin with the first song in your books, 'Silent Night.'"

As their voices lifted with the first lines, Sarah threw up her hands, stepped down and pivoted to face them. When the girls all stopped singing, one after another, Miss Jackson halted on the piano.

Sarah glared at them. "Oh no, not like that! Start out softly and let your voices build up. You all sound sharp."

Linna automatically turned to Eunice, almost as if she was Henry, and grimaced. She was surprised to see exactly the same kind of expression on Eunice's face.

The half-hour practice disappeared so quickly they didn't even get half through the songs. It was, Linna discovered, much harder to be in the choir than she'd thought. She was glad she'd been practising the *lieder* for so long, as her voice was strong and didn't get tired and go sharp or flat like some of the others.

Day after day she sang the words to the each of the eight songs for the Christmas play. Day after day Sarah complained about something one of the girls was doing wrong, or some way their voices weren't blending to create perfect harmonious sounds. But she gradually stopped complaining, as the songs grew stronger and stronger. Often, in fact, she stopped to compliment Linna on something she had done very well. The other girls invited Linna to participate in the outdoor games now, and if she wasn't with Henry, the indoor card games as well. She even ate lunch with Eunice sometimes, before they hurried off to practice.

Papa was in a good mood these days too. After the first taste of really cold weather, it had warmed up again. The crisp fall days meant work was going well on the new houses. Soon it was the last day of November, the saint's day of St. Andreas.

With the dishes finished and put away, Mama and Linna sat at the tiny table, cutting pieces of cloth for a quilted potholder Mama wanted to make Anke for Christmas.

"Weihnachten," Mama said, her eyes glowing. "This is our first Christmas in Canada, and it shall be wonderful."

"But Mama," Konrad asked, "how can we have Christmas without a tree?"

Papa shook his head. "No, there are no *tannenbaums* to bring in with the beautiful smell of Christmas, but there may still be a tree. You will have to wait until Christmas Eve to see."

Linna laughed. She had also wondered if Christmas would feel right without the sight, and smell, of a real *tannenbaum.* "Saskatchewan trees are just bare branches now. How could they ever look green like pines?"

Papa shrugged. "I guess you will just have to wait and see. Tomorrow is December first, the beginning of *Adventszeit.* This will be my first Christmas to share with my family for four long years." He smiled sadly. "I have been waiting such a long time, and now we have so many things to celebrate."

"What about the *Adventskranz,* our Advent wreath? It should be ready to hang on Sunday. Without pine boughs how can we have one?" Linna asked, her mind racing ahead. She wasn't sure what other Canadians did, but she wanted her Christmas to be special, just like it always had been in Germany.

Mama said, "Anke makes her *Adventskranz* of branches wrapped with green crepe paper and decorated with bits of red. I think it could work for us too." She smiled.

"Yes," said Linna slowly, imagining just the right shape of branch for the wreath. "That would be all right. Can I do it this year? Please?"

"Ja," said Mama, "you can prepare the *Adventskranz."* She carefully laid a tiny triangular piece of fabric in the pile they were making.

"Papa," asked Linna, another question popping into her head, "do they have a *Christkindlmarkt* in Qu'Appelle?"

Papa shook his head. "No, not really, but the women from the different churches, and the Willing Workers, sell baking every Saturday at the Parish Hall to raise money for needed things."

Linna thought of Elli going to the *Chriskindlmarkt* at home, and hoped she had made a friend to go with. Surely she would have someone to share the

Zwetschgenmaennle, the spicy *Lebkuchen* cakes, and toys. Linna thought longingly of the streets leading to the market, decorated with their white poles bearing Christmas symbols, garlands of fir and pretty lights, and the centre of the market where there was always a crib, its wooden figures telling the Christmas story.

Mama stood, knelt beside the big bed, and pulled out a small box. "Here are your *Adventskalender.* You'll need them for tomorrow!"

Konrad leapt to his feet, jumping up and down. "Hurray! Hurray! Lucky me!"

"Oh Mama, thank you," Linna exclaimed, throwing her arms around Mama's neck. She had asked Henry about them last week, and found he hadn't ever heard of them, so imagined there would be none this year. "Where did you get them?"

"I only brought the most important things from Germany. These were so small and so needed, that I fit them in."

Linna held the calendar in her hand. Each day during *Adventszeit,* starting on December first and lasting until the twenty-fourth, she could open one of the little doors and receive something tiny, such as a little heart, a candy, or some other surprise, all the while counting off the days to Christmas Eve.

Konrad gripped the *Adventskalender* in his hands, his face glowing. "I can't wait. I just can't wait. Christmas is the best time of all!"

Mama nodded, "Yes, it is the best time of all when we are all together, and God has blessed us with so much."

The excitement among the children in the German settlement built quickly as December began. Konrad rushed home to tell Linna all about the visit of *Sankt Nikolaus,* the Bishop who still found their village even in Canada.

December fifth, the evening of his visit, came on a Monday that year, so Linna hurried through the school day anxious to get back to her own little community for the evening celebrations. Papa too, rushed home as soon as the bank closed, instead of putting in the extra hours he had been doing since the new job began, or working on the new house.

Mama had baked the *Stollen,* or Christmas cake laden with fruit, and the gingerbread. The house was decorated with Christmas pictures, and the *Adventskranz* hung at the door. Although she was helping with building the new house, she had made time for the important Christmas traditions.

Every inch of the soddie had been cleaned in preparation for the feast of *Sankt Nikolaus* on December sixth, with Linna helping each evening when all of the other work was done. Konrad's job had been to clean and polish all of the shoes and boots. He had rubbed and rubbed and rubbed until every one wore a beautiful shine.

"I can hardly wait," Konrad said, as the family hurried through their supper of venison sausage.

"Soon," Papa said, "soon *Sankt Nikolaus* will be here to ask you if you've been a good boy. What will you say?"

Konrad's face grew serious. "Yes, I've helped Mama, and polished everyone's shoes. I worked hard at reading books with Linna, so I am even ready for school!"

Papa rubbed his head. "Yes I guess you are."

Before long someone knocked at the door. Konrad trembled with excitement, his cheeks glowing red. Mama stood from the table and opened the door with a cheery smile.

The bishop, *Sankt Nikolaus,* stood outside; his mule pulled a wagon behind him; there was no snow for a sleigh. A grey beard covered his face, matching his long grey hair, while his flowing white robes draped around his body. On his head perched the high, gold-embroidered mitre. In one hand he carried the big book with each child's name entered, and his crozier, the golden staff he leaned on. He had a lumpy dark sack thrust over his shoulder.

"Have the children in this house behaved themselves?" he asked in a deep voice.

Konrad stepped forward, his body trembling. "I have been very good *Sankt Nikolaus*. I am helping build the new house. I have also learned to read English words..."

While Konrad seemed lost for more to say, *Sankt Nikolaus* reached into his sack and drew out a red-wrapped gift and handed it to him.

"*Danke,*" whispered Konrad, turning and climbing onto Papa's knee.

Linna stepped forward, ready for her turn. "Yes, I have been good this year *Sankt Nikolaus.* I work hard every day at home and at school. I have learned many new things and earned my own money picking wild fruit and stooking sheaves. And I would like to sing for you."

Sankt Nikolaus nodded. Linna began first in English:

O come, all ye faithful
Joyful and triumphant,

Then changed to German:

O kommet, o kommet nach Bethlehem!
Sehet das Kindlein,
Uns zum Heil geboren!

As she sang, Linna imagined herself home in Germany, before the crib for baby Jesus, celebrating *Weihnachten* with Elli, Nana, Tante Karoline, and all the aunts, uncles, and cousins. She knew that must have been where everyone else's minds had wandered too, as even *Sankt Nikolaus* rubbed wetness from his eyes when she was done.

Papa stood and opened his arms; Linna stepped into his hug. "*Danke,*" he whispered, "*danke.*"

She hugged him back.

Sankt Nikolaus handed Linna's gift to Mama, then, said with a quiver in his voice, "There are many children waiting, so I must hurry along. Make sure you are all good for another year."

That night as Linna crawled into her bed in the dark, her shoe set out, waiting to be filled with fruit, nuts, and candy, her heart sang with happiness. While she hadn't found the old Papa with dark curls falling in his eyes, and round merry cheeks, in Canada, she knew this Papa, who had followed his dreams, was still the one she loved.

EACH DAY SEEMED BUSIER than the one before as December rolled along. Linna had little time to spend with Henry, as she ate her lunch quickly each day at school with Eunice before singing began, then, rushed after school to where the new house was quickly taking shape. Henry was busy building sets for the play, painting wall murals with two other boys.

After school one day, when it had snowed again, Henry walked with her to see the new house. The outside was finished, with walls, windows, and a roof, and they were working on the inside. Mama was helping pound nails. The street was almost empty now, but by summer it would fill up with other houses. A few were already framed. Mama was happy that Anke was going to be her neighbour in town, too.

"I'm so glad you didn't have to move away like Kat," Henry said.

Linna nodded. "Me too. Papa likes his new job at the bank. He likes to work with numbers, just like me."

"If you could spell as good as you do sums," Henry teased, "you'd be the smartest student in our class."

"If spelling was as easy as sums, then I could be," Linna said. "But it's not. I guess we're all good at something. You know Henry, Sarah does a good job of directing our choir. We sound much better because of her work. And you are painting beautiful pictures for the sets. I saw them in the library where you had some drying."

Henry beamed. "I like painting. It's fun."

Linna stood still for a second, watching the fresh snow sparkle in the bright sunshine. Like Papa, she was so thankful it had stayed mild enough for building. It was warm, nearly melting, so the snow seemed to be shrinking already. "Winter isn't so bad in Canada either, although I think I like fall best."

"Wait until spring," said Henry. "You'll love seeing the flowers pop up when the snow melts, and the birds all coming back one by one." He stuck his hands in his coat pockets.

Konrad appeared from behind the house. Bending over, he grabbed a handful of snow and rolled it into a ball to throw. "I'm going to get you," he shouted, running towards Linna.

Linna dodged, pretending to run down the street a ways, to avoid the snowball. But instead, she made sure she was within reach of Konrad's throw. "Got me," she screamed, as snow splattered on her coat.

Much to her surprise, when she turned Henry got her too! She stooped quickly, dropped both hands into the snow, and quickly made a ball to heave back at him. Back and forth flew the flying handfuls of snow. Soon her mittens were as wet as if she'd been sticking her hands in the water pail.

At last she stopped, her sides aching from laughter. Konrad tipped over backwards, waved his arms, and announced he was making a snow angel. Linna knew he must be tired from chasing them up and down the street and was really resting.

Much to Linna's surprise, Sarah, her coat neat and tidy instead of dripping with snow and soaking wet like theirs, turned the street corner and walked towards them. "Hello," she said, her voice friendly.

Linna turned to go and pull Konrad up out of the snow before he caught a cold, so Sarah could talk to Henry.

Sarah called her back. "Linna, I want to talk to you," "Me?"

Henry went instead to help Konrad to his feet.

"Yes," Sarah began hesitantly. "It's about choir."

Linna straightened her shoulders, ready for whatever Sarah had to say. "What about it?"

Sarah took a few deep breaths, as though the words she was about to say were difficult for her. "Miss Jackson says the other teachers have listened to us practising and decided our group should be the last ones on the stage, to close the concert. She said I could be the solo singer and the rest of the group could do harmony."

"I'm sure your mother will be proud of you," Linna said, thinking how proud her Mama had been just to have her in the choir.

"I think..." Sarah said, clearing her throat, taking a few more deep breaths. "I think...you have a stronger singing voice than I do." The next words came out in a rush. "You should do the solo. I've already told my mother, and she agrees I'm doing the right thing. Your Papa has talked so much about your dreams to be a singer that she would like to meet you. If you want, when school goes back in the new year, you can come with me to my house after school to meet her."

Linna's mouth dropped. There were too many things to think about – singing a solo – meeting Mrs. Booker. She couldn't find the words to answer.

Henry didn't seem surprised at all, as he drew up alongside Linna with Konrad. "That's very nice of you," he said quietly.

"I'm not doing it to be nice," Sarah said quickly. "I'm doing it because I think Linna has the strongest voice and it will carry best in the Hall."

Henry grinned. "But it's nice anyway."

Konrad stepped up to his sister, and reached for her hand. "I like to listen to Linna sing," he said proudly.

Linna squeezed Konrad's fingers.

"Well," Sarah asked, "will you do the solo, Linna? You'll have to work with Miss Jackson to pick out the song, since it would be yours."

Linna nodded, afraid to open her mouth and say the words, in case everything just disappeared like a dream in the morning. Could it really be Sarah Booker giving her the most important part of the whole Christmas concert? Could it really be Sarah Booker inviting her to go to her house?

"Do you want to come with me tomorrow before school to tell Miss Jackson?" Sarah asked, always the organizer tending to the details.

"Yes," Linna said finally, making it real. "I'll think about the song I want to sing, too." She stared at Sarah, still lost for words, and then said simply, "Thank you, Sarah."

"You're welcome." Sarah turned to leave, then said, "I'll walk home with you, Henry, if you like."

Henry glanced at Linna, then replied, "All right Sarah. See you tomorrow Linna. You too, Konrad."

Konrad dashed off to grab Mama's hand as she emerged from the new house. "Is it time to go home, Mama? Is it?"

Mama nodded.

Happiness bubbled up in Linna until it overflowed. She held both her arms out to the side, as if she were making a snow angel standing up, then, twirled around in a complete circle. Qu'Appelle was the best place in the world!

EPILOGUE

Linna and her family had finished moving their few belongings from the soddie into the new house earlier in the day. Her little bunch of treasures had a new home beside the window in her attic room, where she could gaze at the neighbourhood below.

The big black stove had filled the whole house with warmth, just as it had done in the soddie. But the coal oil lamp sat unused on a shelf, since the electric light in the middle of the room glowed with the light of a hundred candles.

"It's time to go," Papa called, hurrying them all. "Time for Linna's opening night."

"Adeline's," Linna whispered. When she became a famous singer, she would be Adeline Mueller, not Linna. But for now, excitement filled Linna so full she hadn't really had any room for supper. While Mama and Papa walked through the snowy streets, holding Konrad's hand, she hurried ahead of them. At the Town Hall she rushed up the stairs to the front of the room, where all the students were seated according to grade, waiting for their turns. The afternoon dress rehearsal the day before had gone well, but she was still nervous as she climbed the stairs to the stage.

Sarah pulled her behind the curtains, taking some ribbons out of a bag. "I thought all of us in the choir could wear matching hair ribbons – if you'd like."

Linna smoothed the front of the green dress she and Mama had been sewing for the past two weeks, in between getting things finished in the new house. The red ribbon would be lovely, especially all tied up in a bow like Sarah's. "That would be nice," she whispered. "Could you put it in for me?"

"Of course," said Sarah. "Sit down on that chair and I'll do it."

Henry walked to the side of the stage from behind the closed curtains, where he'd finished putting up the sets. "We're all ready to begin," he said, smiling at them both.

From the singing of "The Maple Leaf," everything passed in a blur for Linna. The closer the program came to her class play and the choir's part, the more excited she grew. She tingled all over, feeling calm one minute and scared the next. Her throat grew tight. Her palms felt damp. When she looked in the mirror at the edge of the stage, her face was flushed pink and her eyes glistened. She pinched herself to make sure the night was real and not a dream.

Finally, the grade seven-eight class play began. The choir stood at the back of the stage, singing all eight songs they'd been practising. When it ended, the actors left the stage to a round of applause.

The moment had come.

Linna stepped hesitantly forward, standing alone in front of the darkened room. The stage lights shone in her eyes and she blinked a few times. A baby cried. Someone coughed, distracting her momentarily. Miss Jackson nodded to Linna from the edge of the stage, giving her her note on the piano.

This was her moment, the one she'd been dreaming of for as long as she could remember. She trembled, her heart thumping.

Behind her she heard Sarah whisper, "You can do it, Linna. I know you can."

"Adeline," Linna told herself. "She can do it."

When the music began, Linna opened her mouth and let the words flow from her heart. "O Christmas Tree, O Christmas tree," she sang, while the rest of the choir harmonized. For the second verse, she straightened her shoulders and shifted to the German ones, *"O Tannenbaum, O Tannenbaum,"* for the Christmas tree tradition that had come to the new world from Germany, even before her own arrival.

With each note her voice grew stronger and her heart lifted higher. She was just like her Papa, reaching for dreams.

AFTERWARD

LINNA'S STORY IS FICTIONAL, as are her family and friends, but many of the events in the story really happened in the town of Qu'Appelle, Saskatchewan. I have always lived here, first on a farm when I was small, then in town after I married, so I've always been interested in the story of its early settlers.

Although I've changed the dates of a few events by a month or two, to make them better fit the timeline of the story I wanted to tell, they are portrayed as accurately as I can make them from my community's history book, *Qu'Appelle, Footprints to Progress.*

There really was a German settlement of thirty-four families, who all lived in whitewashed sod houses trimmed with blue, about half a mile south of the railway tracks on CPR land. Since they didn't pay taxes to the town, they were labelled squatters. The Women's

Christian Temperance Movement did have a meeting in Qu'Appelle in August of 1910; the liquor plebiscite, however, was held in December of 1910 rather than October, as described in this story. The results of the plebiscite were the same and the settlers were forced to move or pay rent in January of 1911, rather than before Christmas, as happens in my story. Many bought lots on the east end of Qu'Appelle at a cost of thirty-one dollars each.

The community activities and setting are as described: the Immaculate Conception Roman Catholic Church, the slide show, the town library, the curfew for children and fine for being out without a parent, the stores and hotels, the school, the Agricultural Fair, and the drought of 1910; cyclones also occurred.

Horse racing was held frequently in Qu'Appelle from the 1880s onward, and the town was reputed to have had the fastest track in the Northwest. The Qu'Appelle Sports Club planned races on half holidays throughout the summer around 1910. These commenced at 2 p.m. with bagpipes in attendance.

The fires in Qu'Appelle have been the biggest challenge in its history. The mill, which did supply power to the town, burnt on a Friday in early August of 1910. It was never rebuilt. Many other fine historic buildings were burnt in the past century too, leaving few of the original ones. In 2003, we lost the Queen's Hotel, which had stood for one hundred and twenty years, so the last original building on Main Street is gone.

Finally, I'd like to acknowledge the work of the Qu'Appelle Historical Society: Larry McCullough, Shirley Waters, Jean Kurbis, Melnie Beattie, Eileen Herman, and Bruce Farrer, who compiled *Qu'Appelle Footprints to Progress,* without which I wouldn't have been able to write this story.

ABOUT THE AUTHOR

LINDA AKSOMITIS is the author of *Snowmobile Adventures*, part of the *Amazing Stories* series from Altitude Publishing, and a young adult novel, *Snowmobile Challenge*, which was a finalist for a 2003 Saskatchewan Book Award. A professional writer, she has published over 500 articles in travel magazines, outdoor sports publications and others, as well as doing technical writing, textbooks, courses, and material for radio. She also worked for ten years as a children's librarian.

Born in Regina, Linda Aksomitis has lived in Qu'Appelle for most of her life. She is completing a Master of Vocational/Technical Education degree, and is an avid snowmobiler and outdoor sportsman. You can visit Linda online at *www.aksomitis.com*.

Coteau Books began to develop the *From Many Peoples* series of novels for young readers over a year ago, as a celebration of Saskatchewan's Centennial. We looked for stories that would illuminate life in the province from the viewpoints of young people from different cultural groups and we're delighted with the stories we found.

We're especially happy with the unique partnership we have been able to form with the LaVonne Black Memorial Fund in support of *From Many Peoples*. The Fund was looking for projects it could support to honour a woman who had a strong interest in children and their education, and decided that the series was a good choice. With their help, we are able to provide free books to every school in the province, tour the authors across the province, and develop additional materials to support schools in using *From Many Peoples* titles.

This partnership will bring terrific stories to young readers all over Saskatchewan, honour LaVonne Black and her dedication to the children of this province, and help us celebrate Saskatchewan's Centennial. Thank you to everyone involved.

Nik Burton
Managing Editor, Coteau Books

LAVONNE BLACK

My sister LaVonne was born in Oxbow, Saskatchewan, and grew up on a small ranch near Northgate. She spent a lot of time riding horses and always had a dog or a cat in her life. LaVonne's favourite holiday was Christmas. She loved to sing carols and spoil children with gifts. People were of genuine interest to her. She didn't care what you did for a living, or how much money you made. What she did care about was learning as much about you as she could in the time she had with you.

We are proud of our LaVonne, a farm girl who started school in a one-room schoolhouse and later presented a case to the Supreme Court of Canada. Her work took her all over Saskatchewan, and she once said that she didn't know why some people felt they had to go other places, because there is so much beauty here. LaVonne's love and wisdom will always be with me. She taught me that what you give of yourself will be returned to you, and that you should love, play, and live with all your heart.

LaVonne felt very strongly about reading and education, and the LaVonne Black Memorial Fund and her family hope that you enjoy this series of books.

Trevor L. Black, little brother
Chair, LaVonne Black Memorial Fund

LAVONNE BLACK was a tireless advocate for children in her years with the Saskatchewan School Boards Association. Her dedication, passion, and commitment were best summed up in a letter she wrote to boards of education one month before her death, when she announced her decision to retire:

"I thank the Association for providing me with twenty-three years of work and people that I loved. I was blessed to have all that amid an organization with a mission and values in which I believed. School trustees and the administrators who work for them are special people in their commitment, their integrity, and their caring. I was truly blessed and am extremely grateful for the opportunities and experiences I was given."

LaVonne was killed in a car accident on July 19, 2003. She is survived by her daughter, Jasmine, and her fiancé, Richard. We want so much to thank her for all she gave us. Our support for this book series, *From Many Peoples,* is one way to do this. Thank you to everyone who has donated to her Memorial Fund and made this project possible.

Executive, Staff, and member boards of
The Saskatchewan School Boards Association

Also available in the series

CHRISTMAS AT WAPOS BAY
by Jordan Wheeler & Dennis Jackson

At Christmas time in Northern Saskatch-ewan, three Cree children –
Talon, Raven, and T-Bear – visit their *Moshum's* (Grandfather's) cabin to
learn about traditional ways and experience a life-changing adventure.

ISBN: 978-1-55050-324-1 – $8.95

NETTIE'S JOURNEY
by Adele Dueck

Nettie's story of life in a Mennonite village in Ukraine as told to her
granddaughter in present-day Saskatchewan. From the dangers of WWI
to their escape to Canada, this is a captivating eye-witness account
of a turbulent period in history.

ISBN: 978-1-55050-322-7 – $8.95

THE SECRET OF THE STONE HOUSE
by Judith Silverthorne

Twelve-year-old Emily Bradford travels back in time to
witness her ancestors pioneering in Saskatchewan and
discovers a secret that will help explore her family's roots in Scotland.

ISBN:978-1-55050-325-8 – $8.95

Available at fine bookstores everywhere.

Amazing Stories. Amazing Kids.

WWW.COTEAUBOOKS.COM